KB067474

체스의 모든 것

〈K-픽션〉 시리즈는 한국문학의 젊은 상상력입니다. 최근 발표된 가장 우수하고 흥미로운 작품을 엄선하여 출간하는 〈K-픽션〉은 한국문학의 생생한 현장을 국내외 독자들과 실시간으로 공유하고자 기획되었습니다. 〈바이링궐 에디션 한국 대표 소설〉 시리즈를 통해 검증된 탁월한 번역진이 참여하여 원작의 재미와 품격을 최대한 살린 〈K-픽션〉 시리즈는 매 계절마다 새로운 작품을 선보입니다.

The K-Fiction Series represents the brightest of young imaginative voices in contemporary Korean fiction. This series consists of a wide range of outstanding contemporary Korean short stories that the editorial board of *ASIA* carefully selects each season. These stories are then translated by professional Korean literature translators, all of whom take special care to faithfully convey the pieces' original tones and grace. We hope that, each and every season, these exceptional young Korean voices will delight and challenge all of you, our treasured readers both here and abroad.

체스의 모든 것
Everything About Chess

김금희│전미세리 옮김
Written by Kim Keum-hee
Translated by Jeon Miseli

ASIA
PUBLISHERS

차례
Contents

체스의 모든 것
Everything About Chess

대학의 영미 잡지 읽기 동아리에서 처음 봤을 때 노아 선배는 어딘가 다른 중력에서 사는 듯한 느낌이었다. 외부의 일들에 관심이 없었고 무슨 말을 듣든 반응이 느렸으며 자기 일에만 진지했다. 그러면서도 일상적인 일들에 서툴렀는데, 서툴러서 못한다기보다는 다르게 하는 편이었다. 주민등록증을 잃어버리고 몇 년 동안 재발급 받지 않았다고 해서 우리가 그렇게도 살 수 있어요? 그게 가능해요? 하고 물었더니 선배는 여권이 있잖아, 했다. 애들은 아, 여권, 하며 납득했지만 그것이 주민등록증을 잃어버렸을 때 대처하는 일반적인 방식은 아니어서 뒷맛이 차고 씁쓸했다. 선배는 서울 출신

As a university student in Seoul, I joined an Anglo-American journal reading club. Noah was one of the seniors I met there. He struck me as someone living in another gravity zone. He was not interested in what was going on around him, slow in responding when spoken to, and serious only about his own affairs. He was clumsy even in his everyday life; or, rather, he did things in unusual ways. For instance, he once said he had lost his resident registration card and not gotten it reissued for several years. We asked him if it was possible to live without the card for such a long time. "Well, you can always use your passport," he answered. Ah, of course, a passport, we all agreed. Neverthe-

이면서도 서울에서 자취했고 왜 혼자 사느냐고 물으면 다른 설명 없이, 가족에 대해서라면 기대가 늘 배반당했다고만 해두자, 라고 해서 나를 매료시켰다. 그 밖에 검거나 흰 옷만 입는 것, 잠깐 밴드 생활을 한 것, 여자 선배를 누나라고 부르지 않는 것, 어깨에 문신이 있는 것, 워킹홀리데이를 다녀온 것, 영어를 잘하는 것, 오토바이를 타는 것, 미술에 소질이 있는 것 모두.

그런 선배가 우울증, 정동 장애를 앓고 있다는 것도 사실이었다. 선배는 일정한 간격으로 약을 먹었고, 어느 날은 극심한 무기력에, 어느 날은 극도의 흥분에 차 있었다. 실수하면 지나치게 자책했고 자신을 때리고 할퀴는 버릇이 있었다. 언젠가 세미나 시간에 《타임》지 칼럼의 제목을 "이것은 강아지가 아니다"라고 잘못 읽은 적이 있는데—당연히 그건 강아지(puppy)가 아니라 마그리트 작품에 나오는 파이프(pipe)였다—선배는 우스꽝스러운 표정을 지어서 사람들을 웃기고는, 나중에 동아리방에 혼자 남아 책장에 머리를 쿵, 하고 박았다. 가방을 가지러 갔다가 그 모습을 본 나는 쿵, 하고 마음이 내려앉았는데 선배는 쿵쿵 하고 멈추질 않았다. 그때 동기인 국화가 들어왔고 부주의하게 소리를 내며 뭔가

less, his answer left an uncomfortable aftertaste, since it was not the usual way people dealt with their lost resident registration cards. His family lived in Seoul, but he lived alone. When asked why he lived apart from them, he explained it in a single sentence: "When it comes to my family, let me just say, they've always betrayed my expectations." His answer fascinated me at the time. In fact, I was entirely captivated by him for so many reasons: he wore only black or white clothes; he had been in a band for a while; he never called female seniors "Sister"; he had a tattoo on his shoulder; he had taken working holidays; he was an excellent speaker of English; he rode a motorcycle; he had a talent for painting.

He was also suffering from manic-depressive psychosis. He was on medication, yet would still become extremely listless some days and highly excitable on others. He would be highly self-critical when he made a mistake, often beating or scratching himself. Once in a seminar, he misread the title of an article in *The Times* as "This is not a puppy" instead of "This is not a pipe," a reference to René Magritte's work. He made a funny face to make the people in the seminar laugh; but later when he was alone in the club room, he banged his head against a bookcase. I had gone into the

를 찾았다. 선배가 돌아보자 국화는 "리더스 다이제스트 천해놓은 거 봤어요?" 하고 물었다. 천연덕스럽게, 놀라거나 걱정하는 기색 없이. 선배는 잠시 생각하다가 뭔가 부끄럽고 창피한, 하지만 어떤 열도 같은 것이 전혀 없다고는 할 수 없는 복잡한 표정으로 캐비넷에 있어, 라고 대답했다.

그 뒤 선배는 자조적인 농담처럼 '이것은 ○○이 아니다'라는 말을 자주 쓰기 시작했고 곧 동아리 사람들 사이에 유행어가 되었다. 이건 진정한 순대국밥이 아니다, 아 이건 정말 여름이 아니다, 아 그런 건 얼터너티브록이 아니고 키아로스타미 영화가 아니고, 학생의 권리를 위한 것이 아니고, '국민의 정부'에서 일어날 만한 일이 아니다. 그 아니다라는 말은 부정의 뉘앙스를 띠면서도 권위적이지 않았고 1999년의 세기말 분위기와 잘 어울렸다. 블랙홀처럼 모두를 빨아들여 유사 빅뱅의 상태에서 무언가를 탄생시킬 듯한 밀레니엄에 대한 기대와 불안에 알맞은 것이었다.

선배는 동기나 후배들과는 잘 지냈지만 교수나 선배들과는 자주 싸웠다. 마치 우울한 소녀가 정오의 소나기구름을 좇듯 어디든 그런 일이 따라다녔다. 세미나가

room to fetch my bag, and when I saw him do that, my heart leapt into my mouth. Noah kept banging his head against the bookcase. One of my class-mates, Kuk-hwa, came in and started searching the room for something, carelessly making noises. When Noah turned his head towards her, she asked him, nonchalantly, with no sign of surprise or con-cern, "Have you seen the file of *Reader's Digest?*" Noah seemed to think for a moment, before an-swering, "It's inside the cabinet." The expression on his face at the time was complex, including shame and also enthusiasm.

Afterwards, Noah began to use the expression "This is not a…" frequently, as if in self-mockery; and it soon became popular among the club mem-bers: "This is not a real pork sausage soup," "Ah, this is not a real summer," "This is not an alternative look," "This is not a work of Kiarostami," "This is not for the rights of students," "This is not something that may happen under a democratic government," and so forth. The expression had a sense of nega-tivity, but also was not authoritarian sounding. Fur-ther, it reflected the fin-de-siècle atmosphere in 1999; it suited our expectations and anxieties about the new millennium, which might absorb all things, like a black hole, and create a pseudo-Big Bang that would give birth to something new.

끝나고 콩국수를 먹으러 갔던 어느 여름날처럼. 그날은 같은 동아리 출신이면서 모교에서 강의하는 선배가 참관을 온 날이었다. 콩국수 열한 그릇이 나오고 노아 선배가 아주머니에게 설탕을 달라고 하자 강사가 슈우가? 하고 언성을 높였다.

"무슨 슈가야? 소금이지."

"소금 아닌데요, 콩국수는 설탕인데요."

선배는 덤덤하게 대답했지만 이미 얼굴은 차갑게 굳고 있었다. 그런데도 강사는 눈치가 없는지, 체면을 구겼다고 생각했는지 포기하지 않았다. 소금그릇을 선배 앞으로 내밀었다.

"소금이지, 인마. 애기 입맛이냐, 소금, 콩국수는 소금."

선배는 주위를 살폈고 하는 수 없이 숟가락을 내밀어서 소금을 떴다.

"그렇지. 슈가는 무슨 슈가야."

강사가 좀 풀린 얼굴로 그렇게 말하자 선배가 피식 웃었다. 강사의 얼굴이 대번에 굳었다.

"왜 웃어?"

"아니, 별건 아니고. 드세요, 그냥."

Noah was friendly toward his classmates and ju-
niors, yet often got into arguments with his profes-
sors and other seniors. Like a melancholy girl who
chases after the midday shower clouds, unpleasant
things seemed to follow him around wherever he
went. One summer day, for example, after a seminar, a group of us went out to eat bean noodles. A
senior, ex-member of our club, and incumbent
university lecturer, happened to be there. When
our bowls of bean noodles were set on the table,
Noah asked the waitress for some sugar. The lecturer raised his voice: "What—*Shuga*? You mean
salt, don't you?"

"No. It's sugar. I need sugar in my bean noodles."

Noah said calmly, but his face had turned rigid
and pale. The lecturer seemed in want of tact, or
perhaps he felt Noah had made him lose face; he
would not let it go. Pushing the salt container towards Noah, he said, "It's salt, dude. *Shuga* is for
babies. It's salt, salt is just the thing for bean noodles."

Noah looked around the table and reluctantly
spooned out a bit of salt from the container.

"Yeah, you need salt, of course. *Shuga*? What on
earth!" The lecturer said, his face relaxing. But then
Noah let out a snicker. Immediately the lecturer's
face grew rigid.

강사는 물론이고 다른 애들도 젓가락을 들 수가 없었는데, 그 긴장을 깨고 누군가 후룩후룩 소리를 내며 식사를 시작했다. 이번에도 국화였다. 국화는 열무김치를 아삭아삭 씹으면서 맛있게 국수를 먹었다. 선배는 아직 숟가락을 기울이지도 않았는데, 소금이 콩국물로 떨어져 염도를 높이고 다른 보통의 사람처럼 국수를, 그놈의 콩국수를—그건 그냥 콩국수일 뿐이니까—먹을 수 있게 완전히 분위기가 잡히지도 않았는데 국화는 젓가락을 부지런히 움직였고, 그 움직임을 통해 국화의 무심함이 맹렬히 전달됐다.

"왜 웃냐고?"

"아닌데요."

"아니긴 뭐가 아니야, 어째서 아니야?"

후룩후룩…… 후룩… 목으로 넘어가는 국숫가락의 리듬. 나는 언성을 높이는 강사보다 국화에게 더 신경이 쓰였다. 저번에 목격한 것도 있고 해서 쟤는 정말 대단히 무심한 애가 아닌가, 저 무심함은 어딘가 공격적인 데가 있지 않은가, 생각했다.

"설탕은 슈가가 아니고요, 슈거. 슈가는 뉴슈가 할 때나 슈가고요. 알죠, 사카린?"

"What's there to laugh about?"

"No, no big deal. Please, just go ahead with your noodles."

Neither the lecturer nor the rest of the students at the table picked up their chopsticks. Someone broke the tension by starting to eat, making a loud slurping noise. It was Kuk-hwa again, relishing her food, munching at some young-radish kimchi. Noah was still holding his spoon in midair, not yet ready to put salt in his bowl and not ready to eat the noodles. Those darn bean noodles, nothing but ordinary noodles. Kuk-hwa kept herself busy regardless, though, stuffing the dish in her mouth with her chopsticks, making her heedlessness clear to the others

"I asked you what's so funny?"

"Nothing."

"I know there's something. What do you mean by 'nothing'?"

Slurp, slurp... slurp. It was the sound and rhythm of noodles going down her throat. In fact, Kuk-hwa made me more nervous than the angry lecturer. "Isn't she an awfully insensible person? There's something aggressive in her heedlessness," I thought, remembering what I had already witnessed in the club room.

"It's sugar, not *shuga*," Noah said. It's s-u-g-a-r.

그 일로 싸움이 나고 강사 편을 들며 사과를 종용하던 선배들과 불편해진 뒤 노아 선배는 세미나에 잘 들어오지 않았다. 어차피 그 세미나를 한심해 하던 차였으니까 잘된 일일지도 몰랐다. 그러면서도 동아리방에는 꾸준히 나와서 《타임》지뿐 아니라 《롤링 스톤》이나 《내셔널 지오그래픽》같은 잡지를 읽었고 "인식의 부정이 인식 자체의 부정으로 되지 못하는 한 모든 예술과 철학은 자본을 위한 꽃이 되리라"라는 길고 복잡한 제목의 영어 에세이를 쓰기도 했다. 선배는 집요한 구석이 있어서 그 칼럼마저 마그리트의 〈이것은 파이프가 아니다〉에 대해 썼다. 여러 장 프린트 해서 테이블에 올려놓고 "이제 이것에 대해 이야기하자. 연락 바람. 018327××××"라고 메모지에 써두었다. 나는 줄지 않는 그 페이퍼들을 안타깝게 지켜보다가 나도 독대를 해봐야겠다고 결심했는데, 그건 선배가 무언가 새로운 감각을 느끼게 해주었기 때문이었다. 선배는 좋다 나쁘다 괜찮다 싫다를 넘어, 그냥 '그렇다'고 있는 그대로 이해해야 할 것 같은 사람이었고 누군가를 그렇게 받아들이는 것은 분명 10대 시절의 감각과는 다른 것이었다.

Shuga is from *nyushuga*[1], that is, saccharin. You know that, right?"

Soon a quarrel erupted and all the seniors sided with the lecturer on both accounts. Afterward, feeling uncomfortable with those seniors, Noah seldom came to the seminar. He had not been satisfied with the seminar anyway, so it might have been a blessing in disguise. Nonetheless, he kept coming to the club room and reading journals like *The Times*, *Rolling Stone*, and *National Geographic*. He even wrote an essay in English that had a long, complicated title: "As long as the negation of cognition is not negating cognition per se, art and philosophy as a whole will be the flower for Capital." Noah has his stubborn side and wrote about Magritte's "This is not a pipe" even in this essay. He made many copies of it and put them on the table in the club room, along with a note: "Let's talk about this. Please, call me at 018327xxxx." Anxiously watching the pile of copies that was not dwindling at all, I finally decided to have a one-on-one discussion with him. I felt that because of Noah, I had been able to experience new feelings. He seemed to be a person whom I should accept and understand just the way he was, without judg-

1) A Korean brandname for saccharin.

번역은 영문과 다니는 친구가 해주었다. 하지만 그 역시 2학년일 뿐이라서 그런지 원문이 그랬는지 번역문에는 이런 류의 알쏭달쏭한 문장들만 가득했다. 이미지의 반역을 연기해 반역의 이미지화를 획득해내는 예술이야말로 정말이지 이해불가능의 자기기만이라고 여겨지지 않는가. 허상의 이미지에 가해지는 자본의 가치 있음에 고도로 친숙한, 그 가치 있음의 유통 생리를 테크니컬하게 운용할 줄 아는, 자본의 유통 시스템에 위협적이지 않을 정도의 찌름으로 희롱할 수 있는 자들만이 누릴 수 있는 감각의 젠체 하는 달러 냄새 가득한 파티가 있다. 파이프가 파이프가 아니기 위해 미술관의 금테가 넝쿨처럼 장식하는 호화로움의 스퀘어 속에서 파이프는 파이프가 아님의—결국 상태도 동작도 아닌—무가치한 명사일 뿐 결국 반역은 기대를 반역한 채 있음이다.

반복해서 읽어도 무슨 얘기인지 몰라서 소장철학자가 썼다는 미학에 관한 책을 참고로 읽었다. 책에서는 마그리트의 이 그림을 "가상의 파괴"라는 말로 설명하고 있었다. 그 책도 친구의 번역문처럼 아리송했지만 그래도 '가상'과 '파괴' 모두 마음에 드는 단어였고 친숙

20

ing him to be good or bad, likable or detestable. Accepting someone that way was entirely different from the feelings I had experienced as a teenager.

A friend who had majored in English literature translated the essay for me. Perhaps because she was a sophomore, the translation was full of enigmatic statements—or maybe it was the original text that was the problem. Paragraphs like: "Don't you think art that imagines rebellion by acting out the rebellion of images is in fact the self-deception of the incomprehensible? There are parties that reek of the arrogant dollar, enjoyed only by those who are very familiar with the value of capital attached to false images, who possess the techniques to manipulate the physiology of value distribution, who know how to poke fun at the system of capital distribution, while making sure not to threaten the survival of the present system. The gold rim that frames the square of luxury in the art museum is required to prove that the pipe is not a pipe. The pipe that is not a pipe is in a state of neither inaction nor action, therefore it is a meaningless name to show that the pipe is not a pipe. In the end, rebellion is to rebel against expectations."

Even after reading that paragraph repeatedly, I was still unable to understand it. I decided to refer to a book of aesthetics by a philosopher of the

하게 느껴졌으므로 나는 선배와 약속을 잡았다. 무척 더운 날이어서 선배는 검은 티셔츠가 몸에 달라붙을 정도로 땀을 흘리고 있었다. 오토바이 헬멧을 든 채 형광등을 등지고 나타난 선배는 외계행성에 막 도착한 지구인처럼 고독하고 쓸쓸해 보였다. 그 행성에서 노아 선배를 제외한 유일한 생명체, 단 하나의 이브가 된 것 같아 긴장되는 순간이었다.

"그래, 어떻게 생각하지? 영지, 너는?"

선배는 맞은편 의자에 완전히 몸을 기댄 채 앉았고 영어로 물었다. 나는 아주 인상적이었어요, 하는 말로 시작해서 모두 동의한다고 우물우물하다가 그러니까 그건 가상의 파괴이니깐요, 하고 말을 맺었다. 선배는 눈을 감고 듣다가 고개를 끄덕였다. 표정만으로는 마음에 들었는지 알 수 없었다. 뭔가 무게를 더해야 하는 걸까, 그러니까 좀 더 호감을 줄 수 있는 단어를, 가상이니 파괴니 말고. 내가 다시 입을 열려 할 때 구석의 인조가죽소파에서 뿌드드드 소리가 나더니 국화가 일어섰다. 아무도 없는 줄 알았던 나는 당황했다.

국화는 테이블로 와서 선배의 글을 집어들었다. 선배가 글을 쓰게 된 동기와 내용을 설명하는 동안 국화는

young school. There, Magritte's "This is not a pipe" was explained with the expression "the destruction of the false image." But that book was as incomprehensible as my friend's translation, although I liked phrases and words such as "false image" and "destruction," which sounded familiar. That was why I arranged a meeting with Noah. It was a hot day, and Noah was sweating so profusely his black T-shirt stuck to his body. Holding a motorcycle helmet in his hand, and with fluorescent light behind his back, he looked lonely and gloomy, like an earthling just arrived on an alien planet. The thought made me nervous since I felt I was the only other living being on that planet, like an Eve for him.

"Well, what do you think, Yong-ji?"

Noah asked me in English, leaning back in his chair. I began "I was very impressed" and then mumbled something about agreeing with him on every point. And I concluded with "The whole point is to destroy the false image." Noah listened with his eyes closed and nodded when I finished. His facial expression did not betray whether he liked what I said or not. Should I add something more weighty? Some expressions that would impress him more favorably? Maybe something else than "false image" or "destruction?" I wondered.

간간이 고개만 끄덕였다. 관심이 있는지 없는지 애매했
다. 그러다 말은 곧 끊겼고 신배였는지 국화였는지는
모르지만 누군가 테이블의 체스 박스를 가리키며 체스
나 두자고 했다. 셋이서는 체스를 둘 수 없고 게다가 나
는 체스를 둘 줄 모르니까 국화와 자리를 바꿨다. 그런
데 그렇게 옆자리로 넘어가는 것만으로도 굉장한 소외
상태가 된다는 것을 엉덩이를 들어 옮기는 순간 느꼈
다.

 자리를 잡고 나서도 체스는 시작되지 않았다. 체스의
룰에 대한 의견이 맞지 않았기 때문이었다. 선배가 연
장자인 자기가 먼저 화이트 피스를 잡겠다고 말하자 국
화는 체스에선 그런 건 없다고 응수했다. 그런 건 언페
어하다는 말이었다.

 "그러면 말을 어떻게 정하지?"

 "뽑기로 정하면 되잖아요."

 국화는 체스판을 골똘히 보고 있다가 감정의 동요 없
이, 다만 뭔가를 정확하게 전달하는 사람의 차갑고 딱
딱한 말투로 말했다.

 "그거야말로 언페어인데."

 "그게 왜 언페어인데요?"

When I was about to speak again, a synthetic leather sofa in the corner creaked and Kuk-hwa stood up from it. Since I had thought I was alone with Noah, I felt embarrassed.

Kuk-hwa approached the table and picked up a copy of Noah's essay. As Noah was explaining his motives and the gist of the essay, Kuk-hwa listened silently, only nodding occasionally. It was not clear to me whether she was interested in the essay. After a while, he stopped talking and one of them—I could not tell which—pointed at a chess box on the table and suggested a game. Since I did not know how to play chess, I exchanged seats with Kuk-hwa. The moment I stood up, I learned that one could feel terribly alienated simply by moving over to the next seat.

Even after taking their seats, though, they did not begin the game right away because they did not agree on the rules. When Noah said he would take the white pieces, since he was the senior, Kuk-hwa responded by saying that there was no such rule in chess, and that it would be unfair.

"How then can we decide who gets which?" he responded.

"Well, we can always flip a coin or something," staring at the chess board, Kuk-hwa said in a cold and stiff tone, like trying to convey a meaning ac-

"우연에 맡기는 게 왜 페어야?"

"우연에는 개입이 없으니까 페어하죠."

선배와 국화는 그렇게 뜬구름 잡는 얘기를 하며 한참을 다퉜다. 나는 선배가 화장실 간 사이, 웬만하면 선배 말대로 하라고 국화에게 부탁했다.

"왜? 왜 그래야 하는지 모르겠는데?"

그렇게 말하는 국화의 얼굴은 정말 모르는 것 같았다. 선배가 화장실을 다녀오고 내가 소파에 가서 좀 누웠다 온 뒤에도 페어와 언페어 싸움은 계속됐다. 그렇게 안 맞으면 체스 따위는 두지 않고 집으로 가면 될 텐데 둘 다 아예 판을 엎지는 않았다. 결국 결정권은 내게 주어졌다. 나는 체스의 룰을 알지 못했지만 무슨 게임이든 선을 잡는 사람이 유리하니까 선배에게 맡길까 하다가 충동적으로 국화를 지목했다. 결국 의지도 우연도 아닌 충동이 게임을 출발시켰고 그렇게 체스가 시작됐다.

여름의 늦은 밤, 운동장의 황폐한 잔디밭이 올려다보이는 반지하의 동아리방, 실링팬의 움직임과 라디오, 그리고 체스. 나는 라디오에서 흘러나오는 록밴드의 노래, 미안하지만 난 널 미워하고 미안하지만 난 널 사랑한다는, 이 말 했다 저 말 했다 하는 노래를 따라 불렀

curately without revealing emotional agitation.

"That's really unfair."

"Why is that?"

"How can leaving it to chance be fair?"

"Chance leaves no room for intervention, that's why it's fair."

Noah and Kuk-hwa kept up what seemed to be pointless arguing for a long time. When Noah went to the washroom, I asked Kuk-hwa to let Noah have his way, if she didn't mind too much.

"Why? Why should I? I don't understand."

It seemed that she had genuine difficulty understanding my suggestion. Noah returned and I decided to lie down on the sofa. When I returned after a brief time, their argument was still going. Since they had failed to come to an agreement, I thought, they should just give up on the game and go home. But, for some reason, neither of them gave up. In the end, they agreed to give me the say. I knew nothing about the rules of chess, but I thought Noah should get the first move, since it tends to be an advantage in all kinds of games. But on impulse I ended up saying I thought Kuk-hwa should go first. So in the end, neither intention nor chance started the game, but instead my impulsive suggestion. And that was how they began playing chess.

다. 그런대로 낭만적인 밤이었지만 둘은 미안하거나 사랑하거나 하는 것에는 관심이 없었고 플라스틱으로 만든 기사와 주교와 여왕을 움직이며 서로를 제거하는 데에만 안간힘을 썼다. 그렇게 잘 나가던 체스판은 또다시 위기에 봉착했다. 이제는 언제 이기는가 하는 문제였다. 국화가 아무 말 없이 노아 선배의 왕을 잡으며 선배 졌어요, 하자 선배가 그러는 게 어딨어, 하고 소리 지른 것이었다. 비명에 가까운 소리라서 국화도 움찔했다. 선배는 땀을, 체스가 뭐라고 손바닥이 젖을 만큼 흘리면서 왕을 절대 체스판에서 몰아내서는 안 되고 왕이 잡히기 직전의 상황까지만 만들어서 상대방이 항복하거나 기권하게 만드는 것이 체스의 룰이라고—거의 초인적인 인내심을 발휘해서—설명했다.

"그러면 클리어가 아닌데요."

국화가 선배의 말을 돌려주지 않으면서 말했다.

"게임인데 뭘 상대방한테 결정권을 줘요."

노아 선배가 절망적인 표정으로 자기 얼굴을 손바닥으로 비볐다. 세수를 하듯이 힘을 주어서 달라붙은 불쾌한 무언가를 떼어내겠다는 듯이 세게.

"이제 그만 집에 가자. 전철 끊겨요."

Late that summer night, in the quasi-basement club room with a window from which a withered patch of lawn could be viewed, the ceiling fan whirled, the chess game was on, and I sang along with rock-band music from the radio, which had some confusing lyrics: "I'm sorry but I hate you. I'm sorry but I love you." It seemed like a rather romantic night, but the two of them were interested in neither love nor apologies, only straining to eliminate each other by moving their plastic knights, bishops, and queens. The game went on smoothly —at least until it came to another crisis. This time, the problem was about when to declare the winner. Kuk-hwa captured Noah's king and said, "You're beaten." But Noah yelled, "You can't do that!" Since he almost screamed, Kuk-hwa and I both flinched. It seemed like just a silly chess game to me, and yet Noah felt compelled to explain painstakingly, his skin sweaty, including his palms, as if he were displaying superhuman patience: "The rules say that the king may be driven into a corner but must never be captured; instead, the losing player is given a chance to surrender or withdraw from the game."

"Then it's not cleared," Kuk-hwa said, refusing to put the king back on the chessboard.

"It's not real, it's just a game. Why should one let

내가 채근했는데도 둘은 미동도 하지 않았다.

"이상하잖아요. 그건 좀 웃긴데."

국화가 그런 말로 선배를 또 자극했다. 그러자 선배는 이제 거의 애원하듯이 원래 체스가 그런 것이라고, 체스는 15세기에 체계가 잡혔는데 그 15세기로 말할 것 같으면 콜럼버스가 아메리카 대륙을 발견한 까마득한 옛날이라고 했다.

"그렇게 엔딩을 합의할 거면 애초에 뭣 하러 게임을 하느냐고요."

"원래 체스가 그렇다니까!"

선배는 절망적으로 외치더니 테이블에 와락 엎어졌다. 선배가 그렇게까지 하자 국화도 더는 말하지 않았다. 선배는 얼굴을 감추고 보이지 않는 무언가와 싸우듯이 끙끙대다가 이윽고 낮은 목소리로 나가달라고 했다. 선배를 혼자 두고 싶지는 않았지만 나는 할 수 없이 자리에서 일어났다. 하지만 국화는 나가지 않고 그냥 앉아 있었다. 그리고 차갑지도 따뜻하지도 않게, 나가려면 선배가 나가라고 말했다.

"전철은 끊겼고 택시비도 없어서 여기서 자고 내일 수업 갈 거거든요."

his opponent have the say?" Kukhwa added.

Noah, looking desperate, rubbed his face with his hands, as if he were washing himself fiercely, or as if removing something unpleasant that was sticking to his face.

"It's time to go home, we'll miss the last subway," I urged them, but they would not budge.

"Isn't it strange? It doesn't make any sense."

Kuk-hwa irritated Noah again. Now, Noah, almost imploringly, explained: "It's just the way chess has been played. Chess rules were systematized in the 15th century. It's the ancient century when Columbus discovered the American continent."

"If the players are supposed to agree on the ending, why bother playing the game in the first place?" Kukhwa said.

"I said it's just the way it is!" Noah yelled in despair and threw his torso on the table face down.

Watching this display, Kuk-hwa did not say another word. Hiding his face like that, Noah moaned as if he were fighting against something invisible. At last, he asked in a low voice if we would leave the room. Although I did not want to leave Noah alone in the room, I had no choice but to rise from my chair.

Kuk-hwa remained seated though, and said, neither coldly nor warmly, that if anyone had to leave

"집이 어딘데?"

선배가 고개를 들지 않고 물었다.

"인천요."

"인천까지 택시 타면 얼마 나오는데?"

그렇게 말하면서 선배는 손으로 더듬어 뒷주머니에서 지갑을 꺼냈다.

"5만 원."

국화의 말에 선배가 얼굴을 들었다. 어이가 없고 무언가 의심쩍다는 표정이었다.

"2만5천 원이면 가지 않아?"

"할증 붙어서 5만 원은 있어야 해요."

"아닐텐데, 내가 거기에 친구가 있어서 아는데 2만 원이면 되는데."

"5만 원이라니까요. 내가 거기 사는 사람이에요."

선배는 지갑을 열었다가 다시 닫았고 헬멧을 들고 나가서 그대로 돌아오지 않았다. 나는 그렇게 해서 선배가 집으로 돌아간 데 대해 한편으로는 안심하면서, 다른 한편으로는 당황스럽고 찜찜해하면서 동아리방을 나섰는데, 국화가 따라왔다. 택시비 없다며? 하고 묻자 국화는 직행버스가 한 시까지 있다고 천연덕스럽게 대

the room, it was Noah, not her.

"We've missed the last subway train and I don't have money for a taxi. So I'll get some sleep here and go to my classes tomorrow."

"Where do you live?"

Noah asked without lifting his head.

"Incheon." Kuk-hwa answered him.

"How much is the taxi ride from here to Incheon?"

Saying this, Noah groped for his back pocket and pulled out his wallet.

"Fifty thousand won."

At that Noah finally raised his head. He had a dumbfounded and suspicious look on his face.

"Twenty-five thousand is enough, isn't it?"

"With the extra charge, I need at least fifty thousand."

"I don't think so. A friend of mine lives there, too, so I know twenty thousand is enough."

"I said fifty thousand. And I'm the one who lives there."

Noah opened the wallet, but then closed it again, and walked out of the room carrying his helmet. On the one hand, I was relieved to see him return home that way; on the other, I felt flustered and ill -at-ease when I left the room. Kuk-hwa followed me out, and I asked her, "Didn't you say you have no money for a taxi?" With utter indifference, she

답했다.

"그거 타면 집앞까지 간다."

다음 날부터 선배는 사과를 받겠다며 국화를 찾아다
니기 시작했다. 둘은 미리 연락하지 않아도 어렵지 않
게 마주쳤는데, 국화의 동선이 단순했기 때문이었다.
국화는 점심은 반드시 학생식당에서 먹었고 오후에는
3일씩 도서관에서 근로장학생으로 일했다. 화요일 저
녁에는 과외를 하러 갔고 목요일과 금요일에는 전공강
의실이 있는 문과대 지하독서실을 여닫는 아르바이트
를 했다. 공부는 주로 이때에 몰아서 하는 것 같았다. 갈
때마다 책상에 붙어 열심이라서 복도로 불러내려는 선
배가 애를 먹었다. 선배는 교양강의 교재인『영미의 문
화』를 들고 가서 '영미인의 레저 생활'편을 펼친 뒤 "경기
의 순서는 합의로 정한다. 승부는 체크메이트 상태(왕이
상대 기물에 의해 잡히기 직전의 상황) 또는 무승부/기권으
로 결정된다. 왕은 체스보드 밖으로 나오거나 다른 기
물에 의해 잡히지 않는다"라는 문장 아래 밑줄을 그었
다. 그러면서 국화에게 체스의 시작과 끝에 대해—그렇
다면 사실상 거의 모든 것인데—아는 것이 없음을 인정

answered that the non-stop buses ran until one o'
clock.

"The bus will take me right up to my house," she
added.

The following day, Noah looked for Kuk-hwa,
saying that she owed him an apology. It was not
hard for the two of them to run into each other
because Kuk-hwa's daily routine was quite simple:
she always ate lunch in the student cafeteria and
three afternoons a week she worked in the library
on a work-study scholarship. On Tuesday eve-
nings, she tutored kids, and on Thursdays and Fri-
days, she worked part time, opening and closing
the reading room in the basement of the Liberal
Arts Department building, where the lecture rooms
for major subjects were located. She seemed to
use the time in the reading room to catch up with
studying. Each time Noah went to see her there,
she was so absorbed in her studies that he had a
hard time getting her out of the room. He brought
British and American Culture, a textbook for the liberal arts program, and showed her the chapter entitled "English and American Leisure Life," underlin-
ing some of its sentences, such as one about
chess: "The first move is decided under mutual
agreement. Victory or defeat is determined by ei-

하고 사과하라고 했다. 하지만 국화는 손을 내저었다.

"선배가 말하는 건 미국식이고 내가 하는 건 유럽식이고. 호텔 조식에도 아메리칸 스타일이랑 콘티넨탈 스타일이 다르듯이."

선배는 국화가 그렇게 당당하게 말하니까 뭔가 당황해하다가 돌아섰다. 그리고 다음 날 체스연맹 사이트에서 제정한 체스의 표준 규칙을 프린트해 왔다. 하지만 국화는 자기가 하는 체스는 그런 게 아니라고 다시 잘라 말했다.

"아니라고?"

"아닌데요, 퍼블릭한 게 아니라 프라이빗한 건데요."

"무슨 말이야? 협회에서 인정한 표준 규칙이라니까."

"그러니까 그런 레디메이드가 아니라 핸드메이드 룰이라고요."

대화의 결론은 늘 이런 식이었다. 선배는 논리를 준비했지만 국화 앞에서 그것은 영 힘을 쓰지 못했다. 선배는 그렇게 매일 이상한 패배를 거듭하면서도 어떻게 해서든 사과를 받아야겠는지, 이겨야겠는지 다음 날이면 국화를 찾아갔다. 한 달쯤 반복되다 보니 사과하라는 선배의 말도, 국화의 막무가내도 시들해지긴 했다. 둘

ther checkmate (when the king is about to be captured by the opponent's chessman) or a draw/default. The losing king must not be removed from the chessboard or captured by any other chessman." Then he demanded that Kuk-hwa admit that she knew nothing about how to begin and end the game—which he claimed was in fact almost everything about chess—and apologize to him. But Kuk-hwa waved it away.

"You're talking about the American style of chess; I follow the European style," she said. "Just like the hotel breakfast, you know, there's American style and Continental."

Noah seemed to be befuddled by Kuk-hwa's confidence, and in the end turned around and left. The next day, though, he came back with a printout of the standard rules of chess, as they're posted at the site of the World Chess Federation. Nevertheless, Kuk-hwa said, once for all, that it was not how she played chess.

"It's not?"

"Of course not. Mine are private rules, not public."

"What're you talking about? I'm telling you these are the standard rules approved by the Federation."

"Well, I repeat, mine's not ready-made like them, mine are hand-made rules."

은 여전히 체스에 대해 얘기했지만 정작 체스가 중요한 것 같지는 않았고 체스에 대해 말해야 한다는 의지 같은 것만 남아 있는 듯했다. 나는 그 대화를 들으면서 무슨 대화가 저렇듯 열띠면서도 무시무시하게 공허한가 생각했다. 대체 체스가 뭐라고, 저렇게 싸우는가. 우리 사는 거랑 무슨 상관이라고. 그것 잘하면 밥이 생기나, 장학금이 나오나. 하지만 그러면서도 선배가 마치 목격자가 필요한 것처럼 국화에게 가자고 하면 거절 못한 채 따라나섰다.

그런 만남이 더 견딜 수 없게 된 건 체스 이외의 것을 이야기하면서였다. 국화는 알고 보면 선배가 굉장히 유아적이라고 했다. 자기 말만 떠드는 것, 타인을 박하게 평가하는 것, 그러면서 자신에 대한 평가에는 공격적으로 반응하는 것, 애정을 갈구하는 것, 오토바이를 샀다가 중고로 팔고 또다른 오토바이를 타는 것, 소비에 열을 올리는 것, 거기에는 돈부터 사람까지 다 해당하는 것. 그리고 국화가 가장 못 견뎌한 건 함께 무언가를 먹고 더치페이 할 때 잔돈을 돌려주지 않는 선배의 버릇이었다. 사실 나도 알고 있었지만 차마 말하지 못하고 있던 것이었는데—왜냐면 의도라기보다는 실수 같았

Their future conversations invariably kept ending in this fashion. Noah kept pursuing logic, but it never persuaded Kuk-hwa. Despite Suffering such a strange defeat day after day, Noah would not give up his daily meeting with Kuk-hwa. Perhaps he was determined either to get her apology or at least to win the argument. A month later, both Noah's demand for apology and Kuk-hwa's obstinacy finally began to run out of steam. They still talked about chess, but what really mattered was not chess, but their will to talk about it. Listening to their debating, I wondered: "How could it be at once so heated and so empty? Why do they have to argue like that over a game? What is chess anyway? It has nothing to do with our own survival. It won't feed us or grant us a scholarship." Nevertheless, whenever Noah asked me to go to see Kuk-hwa with him, as if he needed a witness, I was unable to say no and ended up accompanying him.

In fact, their meetings became even more unbearable when they talked about personal things. Kuk-hwa said Noah was a very childish person. She hated so many things about him: his dominating conversations; his chariness in praising others, yet reacting aggressively to others' criticism against him; his thirsting for affection; his buying a new motorcycle and soon selling it secondhand, only to

으니까—국화는 가차 없었다. "선배 그러다 그 돈 모아서 십 사셨어요."라고 해서 선배 얼굴을 달아오르게 만들었다. 그때마다 나는 내 안의 무언가가 파괴되는 것을 느꼈다. 국화가 입을 열 때마다 선배는 힙하고 쿨한 우울한 청춘에서 어딘가 속물적이고 이기적인 흔한 20대로 달라졌다. 그만 하면 화낼 만도 한데 노아 선배는 이상하게 분노에 휩싸이지도 속을 끓이지도 않았다. 선배는 국화를 참아냈고 그렇게 선배가 참는다고 느껴질 때마다 나는 마음이 서늘했다. 그 모든 것을 참아내는 것이란 안 그러면 모든 것을 잃는다는 절박함에서야 가능한데 그렇다면 그 감정은 사랑이 아닐까 생각했기 때문이었다.

밀레니엄을 맞고 다시 여름으로 순환하는 동안에도 우리 관계는 그럭저럭 유지되었다. 새천년의 일상은 그 전이나 후나 허무할 정도로 같았다. 우리의 모든 것을 날려 세상의 온갖 '소유'를 삭제할 듯했던 밀레니엄 버그도 작동하지 않았다. 그저 일상의 연속이었고 다만 놀라운 건 휴대전화 가격이 놀랍도록 저렴해져서 누구나 하나씩 갖게 됐다는 점이었다. 하지만 그런 흐름 속에서도 국화는 무선호출기와 휴대전화 사이에 잠깐 유

buy another one; his excessively consuming not only money but people, and so on. But what Kuk-hwa detested the most was his habit of not giving her the change after they went Dutch on a meal and he had paid the bill. As a matter of fact, I was aware of it, too, but could not bring myself to mention it to him, since it looked like an innocent mistake rather than an intentional one. But Kuk-hwa was relentless: "Noah, keep at it, and you'll save enough money to buy yourself a new house." That remark made him blush. Every time she criticized Noah, I felt something inside me shatter. Whenever she opened her mouth, Noah was transformed from a melancholy youth, who was hip and cool, into a common young man in his twenties who was snobbish and selfish. It would not have surprised me if Noah had gotten angry, but for some reason, he was not furious with anger or upset about it. He could somehow put up with Kuk-hwa, and whenever I sensed his effort to be patient with her, I felt a chill in my heart. Such a high level of patience is possible only when one knows one will otherwise lose everything. If so, perhaps it was his love for her that lay behind the façade of patience.

The first spring in the new millennium turned into summer. In the meantime, our relationship continued, in one way or another. Our daily routines

행한 비운의 상품 문자 삐삐를 계속 사용했다. 전화를 걸어 싱딤원에게 할 말을 하년 삐삐 화면에 한글로 찍어주는 시스넘이었다. 그리고 결과적으로 그 문자 삐삐 탓에 선배와 나 그리고 국화의 이상한 관계는 끝을 맞게 되었다.

그날 우리는 햄버거를 사다가 동아리방에서 먹고 있었는데, 선배가 생일선물이라며 국화 앞에 상자를 내밀었다. 휴대전화였다. 그런 선물이란 나의 상상을 넘어서는 것이었다. 무지갯빛 종이로 포장된 그것을 보면서 나는 실망이라고 하기에는 더 비참하고 상실감이라고 하기에는 그럴 만한 게 있었는지 여부가 불확실한 감정에 휩싸였다. 그러면서도 그 감정을 덮기 위해, 좋겠다고, 이제 편하겠다고 호들갑을 떨었는데 국화는 "이런 거 안 써요." 하면서 다시 상자를 선배 쪽으로 밀었다.

"왜 안 써?"

"삐삐가 좋으니까. 전화 받기도 귀찮고."

"전화야 받기 싫으면 안 받으면 되는 거지. 요즘 누가 삐삐 쓰냐? 좀 있으면 서비스도 안 해."

"안 해도 이거 쓸래요."

그 단호한 태도에 선배는 기분이 상한 것 같았지만

were the same as before, disappointingly. The millennium computer bug that experts said might blow away all of our possessions did not materialize. Life remained the same. The surprise was that mobile phones became so inexpensive that everyone could afford one. In the midst of this new technology craze, though, Kuk-hwa still used her text beeper, that unfortunate product that had enjoyed a fleeting popularity between the advent of the wireless pager and the mobile phone. The user would give their message to the operator over a phone; then the message would be typed and displayed on a beeper screen in Korean. Little did I think that Kuk-hwa's beeper would soon end that strange relationship among the three of us.

One day we bought hamburgers and began to eat them in the club room. Suddenly, Noah held out a box to Kuk-hwa, saying that it was a birthday present from him. It was a mobile phone. It was the kind of present I would not even dream of receiving. Gawking at it wrapped in rainbow-colored paper, I was overcome by an emotion more miserable than disappointment. It could not be called loss either, since I was not sure if there was any grounds for it. Nevertheless, in an effort to hide this emotion, I said in an exaggerated tone of voice, "Lucky you! How convenient it will be!" But

더는 말하지 않았다. 단지 선물을 주고 그 선물을 거절했을 뿐인데 분위기는 무겁게 가라앉았다. 우리는 각자의 이유로 마음이 불편해졌고 침묵 속에서 먹는 행위에만 집중했다. 그러다 갑자기 국화가 선배, 감자 좀 그만먹어요, 라고 불쑥 말했다. 감자튀김을 한데 쌓아놓았는데 선배가 반 이상 먹어치운 것이었다. 선배는 햄버거 포장도 벗기지 않고 감자튀김만 먹고 있었다.

"선배 있잖아요. 그거 다같이 먹는 거잖아요. 그러려고 거기다 부어놓은 거잖아요. 그런데 선배가 자꾸 감자를 먹어서요, 왜 그런지 버거는 안 먹고 자꾸 그것만 계속 집어먹으니까요. 그러면 그럴수록, 제 몫은 줄어들잖아요. 아씨, 나 이거 먹고요, 청량리까지 가서 알바를 해야 하는데요. 선배, 선배가 감자를 다 먹었잖아요. 충분히 먹었는데도 자꾸 욕심을 내잖아요. 그러니까 선배, 그만 먹어요. 제발 그만, 감자 좀 그만 먹으라고요."

선배가 손가락을 들어 입으로 빨았고 다시 냅킨으로 닦았다. 국화는 그런 선배가 정말 마음에 들지 않는지 그게 뭐라고 목소리까지 떨면서 계속 화를 냈다. 선배는 정말 이해가 안 가요. 아니, 감자는 같이 먹으려고 그렇게 해놓은 것인데 어떻게 감자를 혼자 다 먹을 수가

Kuk-hwa said, "I don't use a thing like this," pushing the box back towards Noah.

"Why not?"

"I like my beeper, that's all. And it's a nuisance to answer all the calls."

"You don't have to answer them if you don't want to. Who on earth uses a beeper these days? Soon they'll stop beeper service altogether."

"So be it. I'll still use this beeper."

Noah looked offended, but he didn't say anything else. A present had been given and refused, that was all. It should not have been a big deal. Nonetheless, a tense atmosphere set in. Feeling uncomfortable, for our respective reasons, we concentrated on eating in silence. Then, all of a sudden, Kuk-hwa blurted out: "Noah, you've already had enough French fries." Noah had eaten up more than half of the fries put in a pile for all of us. He had been devouring only the fries, while his hamburger remained wrapped.

"Noah, you see, the fries have been put there so all of us can share. But then you've been eating only them, I don't know why, but you haven't even touched your burger. And you still keep taking fries, leaving less and less for me. For God's sake, this is my last meal before I go all the way to Chongryang-ri to work. Noah, you've already had

있냐고요. 감자는 그런 게 아니고요, 선배 혼자 맛있게 먹고 말라는 것이 아니고 감자는 우리가 다 먹어야 하고 그렇게 같이 먹으면 좋은 건데 왜 감자를, 그러니까 왜 감자를 그렇게 많이 먹느냐고요! 국화가 소리 지르고는 먹던 햄버거를 내려놓고 점퍼를 입었는데 일어서는 국화의 팔을 잡으며 선배가 사과했다.

"미안하다, 감자를 많이 먹어서."

상황이 그러니까 나는 뭐라고 할 말이 없었다. 국화가 화가 난 것은 감자 때문인 것 같기도 하고 아닌 것 같기도 했다. 하지만 뭐가 됐든 저렇게까지 구는 건 아니지 않나 생각했다. 선물까지 준비해 왔는데. 그리고 사과하는 선배는 뭔가. 뭣 때문에 사과를 하는 건가. 감자를 먹은 게 정말 그렇게 미안한가. 국화는 그렇게 사과하는 선배를 뿌리쳤고 무언가를 간신히 참으면서 휙 나가버렸다. 선배는 국화가 나가자 어깨가 축 처졌다. 얼굴에 서서히 무거운 그늘이 드리워졌다. 그건 새파랗게 하늘이 좋은 어느 날 그늘 속으로 뛰어들었을 때 갑자기 닥쳐오는 한기 같은 것이었다. 하지만 그건 감자일 뿐이니까 저러다가 내일이면 만나서 체스니 뭐니 하겠지 싶었는데 그렇지 않았다. 국화는 선배와 그 장난 같

enough of fries, and yet you still want more. Stop it, now—please stop eating the fries."

Noah sucked his fingers and wiped them on a napkin. Kuk-hwa must have hated him so much for having no manners, or something else, because she kept fuming over such a trivial matter, her voice trembling: "I really don't understand you, Noah. We put all the fries there to share. How could you've eaten them up all by yourself? Nobody eats French fries that way. They're not only for you to enjoy, they're for all of us. Because, you see, it's fun to share. Why, I mean, why did you have to hog them like that?" After yelling so, Kuk-hwa put down her half-eaten burger and put on her jacket. When she got up to leave, Noah grabbed her arm and apologized:

"I'm sorry for eating so much of the fries."

In that situation, I did not know what to say. The reason for Kuk-hwa's anger might have been the French fries, or something else, for all I knew. Whichever was the truth, I thought her behavior out of line. After all, Noah had even prepared a present for her. But then I wondered, what on earth was wrong with Noah? Why did he have to apologize? For eating French fries? Kuk-hwa refused Noah's apology, though, and rushed out, looking like barely in control of herself. After Kuk-

기도 하고 뭔가 심각한 논쟁 같기도 한 대화를 더는 해주지 않았고 눈도 마주치지 않았다.

그렇게 사이가 멀어지고 국화가 휴학하고 나서 몇 달도 되지 않아 내 머릿속에서는 국화가 잊혔다. 하지만 술자리가 있던 어느 밤 선배는 나와 길을 걸어 집으로 돌아가다 나는 아직도 국화에 관해 지속된 생각을 해, 라고 잔뜩 취해 더 꼬부라진 영어로 말했다. 걔가 자기는 뭐가 되든 앞으로 이기는 사람이 될 거라고 했던 걸 기억해. 그 말은 나도 기억하고 있었다. 진로 이야기를 하면서 선배는 사실 자기는 뭘 해야 할지 모르겠다고 했고 나는 NGO단체에서 일하고 싶다고 했는데 국화는 난데없이 자기는 이기는 사람이 되고 싶다고 했다. 이기는 사람, 부끄러움을 이기는 사람이 되겠다고. 강심장이 되겠다는 뜻이냐고 했더니 아니 그게 아니고 이기는 사람, 부끄러우면 부끄러운 상태로 그걸 넘어서는 사람, 그렇게 이기는 사람. 정확히 뭘 이기겠다는 것인지는 모르겠지만 국화는 냉정하고 무심하니까 얼마든지 그럴 수 있으리라 생각했는데 노아 선배는 그 말이 뭐가 그렇게 감동적인지 얼굴을 두 손으로 가리며 뭐 그런 말이 있냐, 했다. 어떻게 그런 말을 다 해. 선배는

hwa left, Noah's shoulders sagged. Gradually, his face began to cloud over, conjuring up an image of a person suddenly assailed by a chill on coming out of the warm sunlight—cast down from a clear, blue sky—into the shade. But I reasoned that they were likely to see each other the next day and talk about chess and whatnot as usual, because, after all, it was only about French fries. My reasoning, however, proved wrong. From then on, Kuk-hwa refused to talk with Noah, whether it was simple bantering or serious debating. She even avoided eye contact with him.

That was how we became estranged from each other. And only a few months after Kuk-hwa took leave of absence from the university, I had already forgotten about her. One night, however, after a drinking party, Noah and I happened to walk home together because our houses lay in the same direction. Suddenly, Noah told me in English, in drunken and slurred speech: "I've never stopped thinking about Kuk-hwa. I remember her saying she wanted to be a conqueror." I also remembered that. We had been talking about our future plans. Noah had said he did not have any concrete plans yet. I said I wanted to work for an NGO. Kuk-hwa said she wanted to be a conqueror. She added she wanted to be a person who could conquer shame.

주머니에 손을 넣고 느리게 걸으면서 나는 개가 이기는
사람이 될 거리고 생각해, 라고 다시 말했다. 그래서 나
는 개가 이기는 사람이 되라고 응원해, 정말 확실히 그
렇게 될 수 있을 거라고 생각해, 거기에는 아무런 의심
이 없다고 생각해, 하지만 나는 앞으로 걔를 볼 수 없을
거라고 예상해, 그것은 어떤 오류의 가능성 없이 확실
해.

*

  노아 선배는 대선이 있던 해에 같은 증권사에 다니는,
피비 케이츠를 닮은 미인과 결혼했다. 피비 케이츠를
처음 만나고 놀랐던 건 그렇게 오래 알고 지내온 나보
다 선배에 대해 많이 알고 있다는 점이었다. 만난 지 일
년도 채 되지 않았는데 역시 연애의 열도란, 사랑의 장
악력이란 대단했다. 선배와 지내면서 나는 내가 세상에
서 선배를 가장 잘 아는 사람이라는 사실에 마음을 기
대왔는데 모든 것이 쓸려나간 기분이었다. 그러고 보니
무채색 계열의 옷만 입어온 선배가 민트색의 산뜻한 셔
츠를 입고 있었다. 피비 케이츠가 선물한 옷이라고 했

When asked if she meant to be a bold person, she answered, "No, that's not it. I mean I want to be able to overcome my shame while accepting that shame as part of myself. That kind of conqueror I'm talking about." I did not understand what exactly she wanted to conquer, but being aware of her cool-headedness and heedlessness, I believed she could easily make herself into any kind of a conqueror. Noah, though, seemed to have been not only deeply impressed but also surprised by Kuk-hwa, which baffled me. Burying his face in his hands, he said, "What an amazing thing to say! How on earth did she come up with an idea like that?" Walking slowly, hands in his pockets, he continued, "I think she will be that kind of conqueror. And I'm rooting for her to be one. I truly believe she can be such a person. I have no doubts about it. But I also believe I won't be able to see her ever again. It's a fact, with no room for errors."

*

In the year of the presidential election, Noah married a beautiful co-worker of his, a Phoebe Cates's look-alike, at his stockbrokerage firm. What surprised me the most when I first met the Phoebe Cates's look-alike was the fact that she knew so

다. 나는 사랑에서 대상에 대한 정확한 독해란, 정보의 축적 따위란 그리 중요하지 않다는 것을 실감했다. 중요한 것은 변화의 완수였다.

결혼을 하고 한동안 선배는 나를 포함해 대학 때 사람들과 연락을 끊다시피 하고 살았다. 신혼 생활이 바쁜 듯도 했고 무언가 다른 안정감 속에 살기 시작한 듯도 했다. 처음에는 가슴 아팠지만 차츰 선배를 향한 내 마음도 부피를 줄여갔다. 가장 먼저 선배에 대한 감각—목소리, 얼굴, 체취, 어쩌다 닿았을 때의 몸의 느낌—같은 것이 희미해졌고 다음에는 사실이나 정보 같은 것이 사라져서 과거의 일들이 불명확해졌다. 그때 누구의 생일날 선배가 왔었던가. 그 교양수업을 선배가 들었던가. 그때 선배가, 선배가, 있었던가. 마지막으로는 3차원이라고 할 만한 감각에 공동(空洞)이 생겨났는데 이를테면 이러한 변화였다. 술에 취한 채로 영화관에 들어가 〈나라야마 부시코〉를 보고나서 거리를 걸었을 때 분명 선배와 나 사이를 넘나들었던 감정의 서라운드 같은 것. 그때 우리는 산다는 것의 비참에 몰두해 있었기 때문에 그렇게 되지 않기 위해 당장이라도 무언가 깊숙한 포옹이나 구애의 말을 해야 할 듯한 다급함으로 몸

much about Noah, more than I did, I who had known him for such a long time. They had met for the first time less than a year before. Not surprisingly, the power of enthusiasm shared by lovers— the possessive ardor for one's partner—was boundless. I had always thought I knew Noah better than anyone, which had been a great comfort to me. Now I felt everything had washed out of me. Noah, who had always worn black or white clothes, was now wearing a bright, mint-colored shirt, a present from his wife. It was brought home to me how, when it comes to understanding one's lover, the accumulation of information is not as important as being able to transform the lover.

After he got married, Noah almost completely severed ties with those he had known at the university, including me. It seemed their honeymoon-like life kept him busy, or he had found a new kind of peace and quiet in married life. At first, I grieved about it, but as the time passed, Noah occupied my mind less and less. The senses—his voice, facial features, smell, accidental touching of skin—were the first things to fade away. Next, facts and information about him disappeared, making my memories of our old days inaccurate. Whose birthday party was it that Noah joined? Did Noah take that liberal arts course? At that time was Noah there? In

을 떨었다. 하지만 연락이 끊어지자 그 입체의 기억은 사라졌고 그 일은 그냥 어느 한밤의 수상쩍은 산책 같은 것으로 남게 되었다. 시간의 힘은 대단했고 예외는 없는 듯했다.

그러다 사람들이 노아 선배가 찾아왔다는 말을 하기 시작한 게 재작년 겨울이었다. 우울증이 더 심해진 것 같다고 했다. 선배는 회사를 그만두고 이혼했다고. 이혼을 하고 회사를 그만둔 것일 수도 있지만. 선배를 만났다는 사람이 꽤 많아서 언젠가는 나도 만날 수 있겠구나 생각했다. 그리고 꽃샘추위가 대단하던 날에 선배와 점심을 먹었다. 선배는 날씨에 맞지 않는 얇은 점퍼를 입고 있었고 전처럼 무채색의 옷차림이었다. 나는 변화가 완수된 듯 보여도 그것이 지속을 보장하지 않는다는 사실을 우울하게 곱씹었다. 선배는 몇몇 사람들에게 이미 했던, 그래서 이젠 대학 때 사람들이 다 알게 된 근황을 다시 이야기했다. 확실히 전보다 더 심각한 상황에 놓여 있는 것 같았다. 선배는 말을 한 번에 못 알아듣고 잠에서 막 깨어난 사람처럼 왜, 하고 자꾸 되물었다. 그렇게 눈을 끔벅거리면서 왜, 하고 물을 때 선배는 여기가 아니라 먼 데 있는 사람 같았다.

the end, a hollow formed in what could be called a three-dimensional sense of my memories. For example, the emotional ambiance I believe Noah and I shared when we got drunk once, went to see the movie "The Ballad of Narayama," and afterwards promenaded together in the streets faded. Desperately wanting to emerge from the misery of the life both of us were immersed in at the time, we trembled with our urgent need to do something together right there and then, like embracing each other passionately or saying some words of courtship. Once we lost contact with each other, the three-dimensional memories vanished, and that quasi-romantic evening remained in my memory as only a dubious nocturnal promenade. The power of passing time, I was reminded, is terrible and excuses nothing and no one.

It was two winters ago when people began to tell me Noah had come to see them. They said his depression seemed to have gotten worse, and he had resigned from the firm and gotten divorced. Or he might have gotten divorced first and then resigned. Having heard that quite a number of people had already met Noah, I thought I too would see him sooner or later. And one day, when the spring cold snap was severe, I had lunch with him. He wore a thin jacket, despite the cold weather, colorless as

"너는 잘 지냈냐? 괜찮아?"

나는 괜찮은가 아닌가 생각하다 괜찮지는 않지만 안 괜찮으면 또 어쩌겠느냐고 대답했다. 선배는 고개를 끄덕였고 재밌는 얘기 하나 해줄까, 하고 말했다. 한 번은 하루 종일 사람들을 만나러 다녔는데 다녀와서 보니까 사람들한테 자기 명함이 아니라 다른 사람에게 받은 명함을 돌렸다는 얘기. 그렇게 타인의 명함을 돌리는데도 자기는 물론이고 누구 하나 이상한 줄 몰랐다는 얘기. 나는 어느 맥락에서 웃어야 할지는 몰랐지만 그래도 재밌는 얘기라고 하니까 어색하게 웃어 보였다. 얼굴을 일그러뜨린 것에 가까웠는데 선배는 내가 그렇게 한심해, 라고 했다. 점심을 먹고 회사로 돌아간 나는 평소와 다름없이 업무를 보다 퇴근했다. 집으로 가서 쉬고 싶다고 생각하면서도 무작정 시내를 걸었고 아무 술집에나 들어가 앉았다. 선배를 보면서 느꼈던 새로운 감각 같은 건 다 어디로 간 것일까? 나는 울면서 술을 마셨는데, 술을 마셔서 울게 되었는지, 울기 위해서 술을 마셨는지는 알 수 없었다. 그 뒤로 선배를 자주 만났다. 선배가 먼저 연락하기도 하고 내가 부르기도 했다. 선배는 주로 영화관이나 서점에서 시간을 보냈고 서울 시내를

before, that is, before his marriage. I was forced to ponder another gloomy fact of life: a transformation, even when it appears to have been executed successfully, is not necessarily guaranteed. Noah told me about what had happened to him, which he had already told some other people, so by then almost all of his old friends had heard. He definitely looked like he was in a more-serious situation. He was slower in understanding what I said and kept asking "Why?" as if he had just awoken. When he asked "Why?", blinking his eyes slowly, he seemed to be somewhere else, a place far away from here.

"How about you? You getting along okay?" he asked me.

And I asked myself if I was really okay before answering: "I'm not okay, but then there's nothing I can do about it." Noah nodded, and then said, "You wanna hear a funny story?" And so he related this story: One day, when he came back to his office, after calling people on business, he realized he had given all of them the wrong business cards; those he had been given by others, instead of his own. And not one of them, let alone himself, noticed the mistake. I failed to get the punch-line, but gave an awkward laugh, simply because he had already told me it was a funny story. At my response, which was more frowning than laughing, Noah said, "That's

빼고는 근교도 나가지 않는 것 같았다. 서너 번쯤 만났을까, 선배는 국화를 만나보고 싶다고 했다.

"너는 동기니까 어디 알아볼 데가 없니?"

"없는데, 연락이 다 끊겨서."

내가 그렇게 말하자 선배는 그래, 그럴테지, 하며 청을 거뒀다. 그리고 체스가 두고 싶은데 그럴 사람이 없어서 그런다고 변명했다. 자기는 그래서 하는 수 없이 게임 앱으로 익명의 유저들과 대국을 한다고. 나는 집으로 돌아가 '우리 모두의 체스'라는 그 앱을 다운받아 보았다. 체스 실력이 초급인지 중급인지 등을 정하고 게임창을 만들어놓으면 사람들이 들어와 게임을 하는 방식이었다. 나는 밤새도록 전 세계 사람들과 체스를 뒀고 그렇게 계속 지면서 체스의 룰에 대해 배웠다. 이제 보니 룰은 선배의 것이 다 맞았다. 그건 논쟁의 여지가 없는 것이었고 궁금해할 필요도 없던 것이었다. 그렇게 체스를 알게 되었지만 다음 날 나는 종일 전화를 돌려 국화를 수소문했다. 어떤 애들은 국화가 대치동에서 학원을 한다고 했고 어떤 애들은 그걸 하다가 문제가 생겨 그만두었다고 했다. 연락처를 알아낸 뒤에는 또 이틀을 고민하다가 내가 먼저 전화했다. 국화는 여

exactly how hopeless I am." After lunch, I went to my office and worked as usual. Getting off work, I wanted to go home to rest, and yet I found myself walking around the city aimlessly and ended up in a bar and found myself wondering: "Where have all the fresh sensations gone—those that Noah helped me experience years ago?" I cried while drinking. I had no clue whether I cried because I was drunk or I got drunk so that I could cry. After that, I met Noah several more times. Sometimes Noah called me first, and other times I called him. He whiled away the time mainly in movie theatres or book-stores. He seemed to stay only in Seoul, never venturing out of the city, not even to the suburbs. After three or four such meetings, Noah told me he wanted to see Kuk-hwa.

"You two were classmates, so you should know how to find her."

"No, I don't know how. I lost touch with all of them."

At that, Noah withdrew his request, saying "Of course. I understand." He excused himself by tell-ing me that he wanted to play chess but had no one to play with. In fact, he added, he had decided to settle for playing chess with the anonymous op-ponents on a chess application. Returning home, I downloaded the app, which was called "Chess for

전히 인천에 살고 있었고 자기 동네에 좋은 공원이 있다며 거기서 만나자고 했다. 공원의 이름은 자유─였는데 막상 가보니 비둘기가 날고 노숙자들이 벤치에 누워 있는 그저그런 공원이었다.

국화는 더블버튼의 푸른 투피스를 입고 다가왔다. 화장기 없는 얼굴은 좀 나이 든 것 같았지만 상상보다는 밝은 얼굴이었다. 우리는 벤치에 어색하게 앉아서 이야기했는데, 국화는 내 근황에 대해 거의 묻지 않았다. 무슨 일을 하는지, 결혼은 했는지, 살만은 한지 그런 것에 열을 올리며 캐물은 건 나였다. 알고 싶어서라기보다는 할 말이 없어서였는데 국화는 굳이 말을 아껴서가 아니라 그게 뭐가 그렇게 중요하냐는 듯이 시들하게 대답했다. 강의는 하지, 요즘도. 결혼이 좋은 건지는 확신이 없어 너는 그러면 왜 안 했니. 살지, 잘살아, 나쁘지 않게 살고 있어. 나쁘면 또 얼마나 나쁘다고, 하는 식이었다. 그만 갈까 싶을 때쯤 국화의 휴대전화가 울렸고 나는 농담 삼아 "이제 문자 삐삐 안 써?" 하고 물었다. 국화는 그때 그 일을 다 잊어버렸는지 갸웃하다가 아아 ─ 하고 고개를 끄덕였다.

"그거 참 좋았는데 우리 부모가 문맹이라서 부모 말

All." The first step was to choose a level, such as beginner's or intermediate. After that, a window was set up, and other people came in to play. Throughout the night, I played with people from all over the world, losing one game after another. It was my way of learning the rules. Only then did I realize that Noah understood the rules. There had been no need at all to debate or investigate in the first place. And I learned how to play chess that night. Then I spent the whole next day making countless phone calls to find out Kuk-hwa's whereabouts. Some respondents said she was running an academy in Daechi-dong, while others said she had already closed the academy owing to problems. Even after I got her phone number, I agonized for two days before finally calling her. She was still living in Incheon and said she would meet me in a park near her place. I was impressed by its name: Freedom Park. When I went there, however, it was just an ordinary park, with pigeons flying around and homeless people sleeping on the benches.

Kuk-hwa walked towards me in a blue double-buttoned, two-piece suit. Wearing no make-up, she looked a bit older, but more cheerful than I had expected. We sat on a bench awkwardly and began talking. Kuk-hwa hardly asked about my life

이 그렇게 한글로 찍히는 게 신기하고. 지금은 없어졌지. 아무도 그런 거 안 쓰지. 그러고 보면 세상이 딱히 더 좋아지는 건 아니야."

선배 얘기를 먼저 꺼낸 건 국화였다. 선배는 잘 지내느냐고 물었고 나는 여러 가지 대답을 떠올렸다가 그렇지 않다고 사실대로 말했다. 우리 사이에는 말이 또 끊겼다. 그러다 국화가 선배에 대해 오랫동안 자주 생각했다고 말을 이었다. 학원이 문을 닫고 한동안 지긋지긋하게 빚에 시달리던 시절에.

"내 딴에는 영리하게 한다고 했는데, 그게 또 그렇게 되더라고. 나는 이런 얘기를 이제 이렇게 웃으면서 해. 내가 이렇게 한심해."

국화는 그때 죽을까, 생각했었고 실제로 그런 충동에 시달리다가 자살 방지를 위한 핫라인에 전화를 걸기도 했는데, 주민등록번호가 뭡니까, 하고 물어서 일순간 분노감에 휩싸였다고 했다. 그 분노감은 아주 강력한 것이었고 모욕을 동반했다. 그리고 그 모욕을 살기 위해 씹어 삼켜야 했을 때 국화는 선배의 이야기를 떠올렸다. 선배가 국화에게만 해준 워킹홀리데이로 외국에 나갔을 때에 관한 이야기.

in later years. I, on the other hand, asked her many questions: What kind of work she did, if she was married, if she was okay, and the like. Not that I really wanted to hear the answers—I just had nothing else to say to her. Kuk-hwa, on her part, gave only halfhearted answers, not because she was being cautious, but she seemed to think our questions and answers were not that significant. "I'm still teaching... I'm not sure if marriage is desirable... Why, then, aren't you married?... Of course, I'm fine. I'm getting along well enough. My life isn't that bad." she said apathetically. I was about to say goodbye when her mobile rang. As a joke, I asked, "You don't use that text beeper anymore?" Kuk-hwa tilted her head to one side, as if she had forgotten all about it. Soon, she nodded her head, saying "Ah!"

"That beeper used to be a very convenient tool. My parents are illiterate, so I was amazed to see whatever they said turning into text messages. Those beepers are no more. Nobody uses a thing like that now. Come to think of it, though, the world isn't necessarily getting better."

It was Kuk-hwa who mentioned Noah first, asking me about him. I thought of various scenarios as an answer, at first, but in the end told her the truth. Silence fell between us again. After a minute or

선배는 외국의 농장에서 일하다가 도둑 누명을 쓴 적이 있었다. 선배는 전혀 모르는 일이었지만 한국인 조장은 그냥 잘못을 인정하고 넘어가자고, 다른 한국인들까지 피해를 본다고 선배를 설득했다. 결국 조장은 선배를 농장주에게 데려갔고 선배는 어차피 연기일 뿐이니까 머리를 숙이고 사과를 했다. 농장주는 넌 언제나 교체될 수 있어, 선수는 많으니까, 너 같은 경우에는 더이상 기회를 안 줄 수도 있어, 하며 화를 냈다. 그건 연기이고 가짜인데도 그렇게 막상 농장주 앞에 서니까 선배는 공포와 수치심에 몸을 떨었다. 그래서 자기도 모르게 두 손을 빌듯이 맞잡으며 용서를 구했다. 그렇게해서 일은 해결되었는데 막상 귀국하고 나자 그때의 모욕감이 선배를 더 집요하게 괴롭혔다. 선배는 그런 기억에서 자신을 구하고 싶었지만 동시에 자신을 벌주고 싶었고 그렇게 벌주고 싶으니까 종종 자신을 학대했다. 나는 그 이야기를 들으면서도 나는 왜 그것을 알지 못하고 국화가 알고 있는가를 생각했다. 이야기 속 선배는 너무나 안쓰럽지만 그래도 왜 나는 아닌가. 내가 알았다면 언젠가의 국화처럼 부끄러움을 이기는 사람이되겠다는 말로, 선배가 그렇게 되기를 빌어줄 수 있었

two, Kuk-hwa said she had often thought about Noah, especially while she was harassed with debts after her academy business failed.

"I thought I was very clever. But then it happened. As you can see, I talk about it with a smile on my face... truly hopeless person that I am."

Kuk-hwa said she had thought about committing suicide at the time. When she was about to succumb to that impulse, she called a suicide prevention hot line. But the moment she heard, "Tell me your resident registration number, please," she was consumed with a surge of fury, a powerful rage fueled by a sense of humiliation. When she had no choice but to suppress the emotional outburst in order to stay alive, she remembered what Noah had told her. It was a story about Noah himself during his working holidays in a foreign country. Kuk-hwa was the only one who had ever heard the story from him.

Noah had been falsely accused of stealing while working on a farm in the foreign country. Although he had had nothing to do with it, the Korean foreman convinced him to pretend he was guilty and quickly settle the affair, because otherwise it could damage the reputations of the other Korean workers there. In the end, the foreman took Noah to the farm owner. Noah thought it was just an act, so he

을까 생각했다. 그 이기는 것에 대한 간절함을 감각할
수 있었을까.

　나는 돌아와 선배에게 국화의 연락처를 알려주었다.
선배는 한동안 국화를 만나러 다녔다. 둘은 그때 그 자
유―라는 공원에서 만난다고 했다. 나는 선배와 국화
사이의 일에는 무심하려 노력했지만 한 번은 참지 못하
고 만나서는 대체 뭘 해? 하고 물었다. 선배는 당연하다
는 듯 우리는 체스를 둬, 라고 대답했다.

*

　오랜만에 만난 선배는 시카고 출장을 다녀오는 길이
었다. 공항에서 바로 왔다며 캐리어도 들고 있었다. 그
동안 연락을 잘 받지 않은 건 나였다. 선배가 더 이상 국
화를 만나러 가지 않게 된 시기와 맞물렸다. 나는 선배
가 국화와 재회했을 때가 아니라 그 재회를 계속 이어
가지 못했을 때 우리의 관계도 완전히 끝이 났다고 생
각했다. 관계의 끝이란 그렇게 당사자 사이의 어떤 문
제 때문이 아니라 당사자들과 제삼자 사이에도 오는 것
이었다. 우리는 어느 때보다도 조용히 전골집에 앉아

bowed his head and apologized. The furious farm owner said, "Guys like you can always be replaced. There are plenty of replacements waiting. I may not give another chance to a man like you." Although it was just an act, a fake, once he was standing in front of the farm owner, Noah shuddered with fear and shame all the same, and in spite of himself he pleaded for forgiveness, pressing his hands together. His performance worked and helped settle the matter at the time. When he returned to Korea, though, the humiliation he had suffered then persisted and tortured him more severely than ever. He wanted to free himself from the memory, yet at the same time he wanted to punish himself. So he often treated himself cruelly. While I was listening to the story, all I could think of was why Kuk-hwa, not I, was the one who had been told the story. I felt deeply for Noah in the story. Why not I? If I had been told, I wondered, would I have been able to say that I wanted to be a person who could conquer shame, as Kuk-hwa had done, as a way to encourage Noah to overcome his shame? Could I have perceived Noah's dire need to conquer shame?

Returning to Seoul, I called Noah and gave him Kuk-hwa's phone number. Noah went to see Kuk-hwa. I was told the two met in the same park, and

있었다. 눈앞의 전골이 우리보다 더 높은 온도로 끓고 있는 것이 아닐까 하는 생각이 들 정도로. 나는 전골이 빨리 끓고 그것을 나눠 먹고 시시한 얘기나 하다가 헤어져 잊어버리고 싶었다. 선배는 내내 바쁘다가 하루 시간이 나서 시카고미술관과 야구장을 다녀왔다고 했다. 미술관에서 〈이것은 파이프가 아니다〉를 직접 보았고 내게 줄 선물로 '이것은 파이프가 아니다'라고 쓰여 있는 파이프를 샀다. 나는 그 나무 파이프를 만져보았다. 니스칠을 했는데도 어딘가 촉감이 거칠거칠했다.

"가루담배를 하나 사야겠네."

"요즘도 많이 피우니?"

"죽지 않을 만큼만 피워."

그리고 우리는 부동산과 차이나펀드에 대해 이야기했다. 선배가 VVIP에게만 제공되는 정보지를 담당한다고 해서 나는 나도! 나도! 하고 외쳤다. 선배는 그런 정보를 안다고 다 돈을 벌 수 있지는 않다고, 자기도 차명으로 투자해봤지만 실패했다고 했다. 그래도 해볼게, 해볼게, 딱히 그렇게 생각하지도 않으면서 나는 그것 이외에는 할 말이 없어서 그 말만 되풀이했다.

식당에서 나와 선배는 괜찮으면 한 정거장 정도 걷지

continued to do so often for some time. I tried not to meddle; nevertheless, once I failed to restrain my curiosity and asked him, "What on earth do you two do together?"

Noah replied, matter-of-factly, "We play chess."

*

I had not met Noah for a long time when I encountered him on his way back from a business trip to Chicago. He still had his carrier with him, saying that he was coming directly from the airport. I had begun to neglect keeping touch with him, which coincided with the time he stopped seeing Kuk-hwa. I thought my relationship with him had ended for good, not at the time of his reunion with Kuk-hwa, but when he failed to keep up his renewed relationship with her. When a relationship ends, for whatever reason, the relationship between the couple and a third party sometimes also comes to a close. Soon we were sitting in a restaurant specializing in beef casserole. We were quieter than ever, silently watching the pot of casserole seething in front of us. The casserole seemed to have more liveliness than either of us. I wanted the casserole done quickly; I could not wait until we finished eating, talking about some silly things, say-

않겠냐고 했지만 나는 싫다고 했다. 너무 춥다고.

"추워?"

"응, 너무 추워."

선배는 내 거절을 이해한다는 듯이 고개를 끄덕였고 돌아서다가 내가 시카고에서 강정호를 봤거든, 했다.

"강정호?"

"야구선수 강정호 알지? 지금 거기 메이저리그에서,"

"아아, 직관했어? 재미있었겠네."

그날 강정호는 등판하지 않았다. 선배는 9회까지 기다렸지만 끝내 활약을 보지 못한 채 경기장을 나왔다. 그때는 이미 해가 지고 난 뒤였다. 선배는 관람을 마치고 나오는 백인 군중과 함께 지하철역으로 향했다. 꽤 먼 거리였고 더구나 경기장 주변은 시카고에서도 악명 높은 슬럼가여서 불안했다. 그래도 선배는 사람들이 이렇게 많으니 괜찮겠지, 하고 생각했다. 하지만 중간쯤 가자 군중은 모두 경기장 외곽에 설치된 주차장으로 향했고 선배만 남았다. 모두들 차를 가지고 있었고 선배처럼 슬럼가를 가로질러야 하는 외국인, 여행자, 이방인은 없었다. 휴대전화 배터리도 다 닳아 불안한 가운데 선배는 길을 헤맸다. 숨이 가빠오고 땀이 흐르는 공

ing goodbye, and finally forgetting about our meeting altogether. Noah said he had been able to take off a day from his busy schedule to visit the Art Institute of Chicago and Wrigley Field. He saw first-hand "This is not a pipe" at the institute and bought a souvenir for me: a pipe with "This is not a pipe" inscribed on it. I held the wooden pipe in my hand. Its varnished surface, for some reason, felt rough.

"I'm gonna buy some pipe tobacco," I said.

"Still smoking a lot?" he asked.

"Yes, but not to the point of risking my life."

Then we talked about the real estate business and the China Fund. When Noah said he was in charge of a financial intelligence periodical for the VVIP, I cried out, "Me too! Me too!" Noah went on to say that obtaining intelligence did not always lead to moneymaking, and that he had once invested under an assumed name, only to fail. "Still, I'll give it a try, I will." In fact, I had no intention of doing so, but having nothing else to say, I kept repeating that I would.

Leaving the restaurant, Noah suggested that we walked together to the next bus stop, but I said it was too cold.

"Are you cold?"

"Way too cold."

황을 다시 느꼈을 정도였다. 음악소리가 불길할 정도로 크게 들리는 허름한 집들과 호객하는 매춘녀, 골목에 모여 있는 어린 흑인들 사이를 통과하는 선배를 한 부랑자가 붙들었다. 야구를 봤니, 네가 응원하는 팀이 확실히 이겼겠지. 네 얼굴이 이긴 사람의 얼굴이라서. 나는 배가 고파. 넌 이겼지만 난 게임에서 완전히 지고 말았거든. 하지만 빠져나가는 법은 내가 알지. 달러를 주면 길을 가르쳐줄게.

"돈을 좀 줘서라도 얼른 떼어내지 그랬어."

나는 이야기를 들으면서 어쩐지 선배의 그 불안에 전염된 것처럼 날카로워졌다. 어쩌면 추워서 그랬는지도 몰랐다. 그런 기색을 느꼈는지 선배는 "줬지, 줬어, 한 오 달러쯤." 하고 말을 정리했다. 돈을 공손히 받은 부랑자는 술을 마셔서 그런지 바들바들 떠는 손으로 길을 가르쳐줬지만 선배는 그 길로 가지 않았다. 거기가 정말 지하철역과 연결되어 있는지 믿을 수 없었으니까. 그렇게 다른 길을 가는 선배 귀에 부랑자가 흥얼거리는 노래가 들려왔다. 런던 브리지 폴링다운, 폴링다운, 하는 노래였다. 배웅하는 것 같기도 하고 뭔가를 예고하는 것 같기도 한 노래. 어린시절 장난감이나 놀이기구

Noah nodded as if to say my refusal was okay with him. He was about to turn around, then he said, "I've seen Kang Jung-ho in Chicago."

"Kang Jung-ho?"

"Yeah, Kang Jung-ho the baseball player, you know him, right? Now, he's a member of the Major League baseball team there."

"Ah! So did you go see a game? It must have been a lot of fun."

On the day Noah had gone to the baseball game at Wrigley Field, Kang Jung-ho had not come to the mound. Noah waited until the ninth inning to no avail. By the time he left, the sun had already set. He had walked toward the subway station along with a crowd of Americans, all leaving after the game. It was quite a distance, and in the vicinity of the field were slums notorious even in Chicago. He felt uneasy, but did not worry much since there were so many people around him. Halfway to the subway station, however, the crowd headed for the parking lots, leaving Noah alone. They all had cars and no one like him, a foreigner, traveler, outsider, had to walk through the slums. To make matters worse, the battery of his mobile was almost dead. Noah anxiously walked about. Before long, panting and sweating profusely, he felt his old panic disorder acting up. Passing by shabby houses, from

의 전자음으로 들었던 노래.

우리는 헤어졌고 나는 택시를 잡았다. 택시는 도시를, 정해진 루트를, 선배에게서 점점 멀어지는 거리를 열심히 계산하면서 달렸다. 그러는 동안 어떤 감각이 끊임없이 나를 일깨우며 선배에게 무슨 말을, 아무 말이라도 해야 한다고 충동질했다. 전화를 걸어보니 선배는 아직도 걷고 있었다. 오늘은 걸어야 할 것 같아서 그러고 있다고. 선배는 미안해, 하고 사과했다. 나는 그런 말은 하지 말라고 했다. 달리 할 말이 있어야지, 하는 선배에게 나는 그렇게 다시 만나 체스를 이겼느냐고 물었다. 선배는 국화 얘기가 나오자 아무 말 없이 더 빨리 걸으면서—도망치는지 달려가는지 알 수 없지만—캐리어의 바퀴소리가 급해지도록 걸으면서, 한 번도 이긴 적이 없다고 대답했다. 체스에 관해서는 자기가 다 틀렸던 것 같다고.

"아니 그렇지는 않았어."

"아니야, 한심했어."

"아니 그렇지는 않았어. 그 정도는 아니었어."

우리는 구제불능의 술꾼들처럼 같은 말만 되풀이했다. 그렇게 말할 때마다 체스는 체스였다가 체스가 아

which loud and aggressive music was blaring, through beckoning prostitutes and a group of black youths in an alley, he was suddenly grabbed by a bum. "Did you watch the ball game? Your favorite team must have won. You've got that winner's face. I'm hungry. You've won, but I've lost a game, dead broke. But, you see, I know a way out of this place. Give me some dough and I'll show you the way out."

"Why didn't you give him some money and get rid of him?" I asked Noah.

Listening to him, his anxiety had somehow rubbed off on me and I had become nervous. Or, maybe the cold weather had gotten to me. Perhaps he sensed my nervousness; he reassured me, saying, "I did, I did give him about five dollars." The beggar received the money politely and pointed the way with a hand that was trembling, probably from heavy drinking. But Noah did not take that way, unable to believe it really led to the subway station. Setting out in a different direction, Noah heard from behind the bum crooning a song: "London Bridge is falling down, falling down, falling down..." It seemed the bum meant to see him off with the song; but it also felt like the guy was warning him against something. Noah remembered hearing the melody as a child, coming from the

닌 것이 되었다가 결국 그것이 무엇인지를 따질 필요도 없는 모든 것이 되어갔다. 나는 아무리 체스에 대해 말한다 해도 결국 아무것도 달라지지는 않으리라 독하게 생각하면서도 말을 멈출 수는 없었다. 그것이 우리의 모든 것이 아니었다고는. 차가운 아이스크림을 삼키듯 치밀어오르는 무언가를 자꾸 밀어 넣고 있는 지금은.

electronic sound box of a toy or game.

We said goodbye and I took a taxi home. The taxi ran through the city along a known route, as I assiduously calculated the growing distance away from Noah. In the meantime, a feeling began to grow inside me, and kept urging me to talk to Noah, about something, anything. When I finally called Noah, he was still walking. He explained that he needed a long walk that day. "I'm sorry," he said, and I told him not to say such a thing. "But, I've nothing else to say," he confessed. I asked if he had ever won any of the chess games he had played with Kuk-hwa after their reunion. At the mention of Kuk-hwa, he became silent and I could hear him begin to walk faster. I was unable to tell if he was making his escape or simply running, but I could hear the wheels of his luggage carrier picking up speed. Eventually, he answered he had never won, not even once. And he added, as far as chess was concerned, he might have been wrong all along.

"No, you weren't wrong."

"Yes, I was. I was completely hopeless."

"No, you weren't wrong. At least, not to that extent."

We kept repeating the same phrases as if we were two irredeemable drunkards. With each repetition, chess seem to be transformed things: at first it was the game of chess, and then something beyond chess, and, finally, anything and all things, no longer requiring analysis or scrutiny. Although I was entirely convinced that no matter how much we talked about chess, nothing would ever change, I found myself unable to stop talking about it. I could not bring myself to say that, in fact, it did not mean everything to us. At least not now, not when I was trying to press down something—as if I were gulping down cold ice cream—that was surging up in me.

창작노트
Writer's Note

k

오늘 눈을 떴을 때부터 하루 종일 무언가와 이별을
한 기분이었는데, 내게 이별을 말한 사람은 한 명도 없
고.「체스의 모든 것」을 쓰는 동안에는 내내 누군가와
체스를 두는 기분이었는데, 내가 한 것이라고는 매일
카페에 나와 일정한 시간 앉아 있었던 것. 물론 체스에
대해 써야 하니까 체스를 배우기는 했다. 한 달 동안 같
은 카페, 같은 시각에 친구와 만나 체스를 뒀다. 우리는
두 시간 동안 체스에 대해 이야기하면서 어느 날은 정
말 안부마저 묻지 않고 체스만 두기도 했다. 그러고 나
서 각자 집으로 돌아간 뒤에 페이스북 메신저로 그런데
어쩌다 보니 체스만 뒀네, 다음번에는 근황 이야기도

From the moment I opened my eyes this morning, and throughout the day, I have felt like I have parted with something or from someone. But so far no one has actually said farewell to me. All the time I was writing "Everything About Chess" I felt as if I were playing the game with someone. In reality, though, all I did was write in a café for a number of hours every day. Of course I learned how to play chess before writing the story because the story was about that game. In the same café, for a month, I regularly met and played chess with a friend of mine. Some days, we talked about the game for two hours; sometimes we got down to playing as soon as we met, without even inquiring

하면서 체스를 두자, 이렇게 말하고 나서 그 다음 주에 만나면 또다시 체스에 관해서만.

그렇게 해서 나는 체스의 기물들을 어디에 놓아야 하는지, 폰과 룩과 나이트와 비숍과 킹과 퀸이 움직일 수 있는 방향에 대해서 배웠지만 소설을 쓰면서 생각해보니 그런 세세한 것들에 대해서는 알 필요가 없었어. 나는 어떻게 해도 킹이 체스판을 떠나지 않는다는 것과, 체크메이트 상황에서 합의나 항복을 통해 승부를 결정짓는다는 사실에 얼이 나가 있었거든. 그리고 체스를 두면서 내가 2014년 여름, 마음이 힘들었던 시절에 대해 말했을 때 친구가 아무 위로를 해주지 않았다는 사실에도. 친구는 그런 불행에 익숙하고 좀 진저리가 나는 얼굴을 하고 있었는데, 돌아오지 않는 위로의 상황에 당황하면서도 나는 그냥 체스를 두었다. 생각해보면 나도 친구가 불행했을 때 도와준 것이 없고.

하지만 그 시간들이 마냥 무의미하지는 않았다. 어찌되었든 나는 이 소설을 썼으니까. 나를 가르치느라 각각의 기물을 직접 그림 카드로 만들어서 설명해주고 싫증을 잘 내는 내가 오늘은 체스 대신 그냥 놀까, 했을 때 그러면 컴퓨터랑 한번 해볼래, 하며 노트북을 켜준 친

after each other, and kept at it until we left. When we returned home, I would get on the Facebook Messenger and say to him, "It's just occurred to me that we played chess the whole day today. Next time, besides playing chess, let's have a chat—you know, about what's going on in our lives these days, things like that." But then the following week we would again talk only about chess.

That's how I learned where to place each piece on the board and the directions the pawns, rooks, knights, bishops, kings, and queens could move. Nevertheless, while I was actually writing the story, I came to realize that I did not need all that detailed knowledge. Nevertheless, I was fascinated with the fact that a king can never, under any circumstances, be taken off the chessboard and that in checkmate, the winner is determined by either mutual agreement or when the losing player surrenders.

I was also taken aback by my interaction with this friend and his aloofness. While we were playing, I talked with him about the painful feelings I had suffered in the summer of 2014.[1] He offered no words

1) Sewol Ferry Disaster: On the 16th of April in 2014, Sewol ferry sank on its way to Jeju Island from Incheon. Out of the 476 people on board, 304 perished, including over 250 high school students on their school trip. It has been said that the illegal enlargement of the ship, freight overload, and absence of emergency measures and training were the root causes of the tragedy.

구에게는 미안하지만 나는 그 시간 동안 막상 체스에 대해서는 생각하지 못했어. 그 대신 이런 것에 대해서 맹렬히 생각했다. 마침 우리가 체스를 둔 곳이 졸업한 대학의 앞이라서 그런 것들을 떠올리기 적당했지.

나는 그 시절 친구가 머리를 어깨까지 기르고 왜 그런지 발목까지 오는 카키색 바바리만 고집하며 시에 대해 이야기했던 것을 기억했다. 친구가 나무판에 새긴 체 게바라 얼굴도 선명하게 떠올렸다. 체는 베레모를 쓰고 수염을 기르고 있었지. 우리는 예수와 닮은 얼굴이라고 말했고 그런 삽화를 초고에 쓰기도 했지만 나중에는 지우고 말았다. 소설의 앞부분을 힘들게 썼고 여러 번 지웠기 때문에 왜 지워야 했는지는 기억이 나지 않지만 막 여름이 시작되는 5월이라 차가운 커피를 마시기 시작했다는 것은 생생해. 그렇게 차가운 것을 삼키면서 나는 무언가를 자꾸 밀어 넣고만 싶었지. 생각하지 않을 수 있다면 얼마나 좋을까. 그러니까 우리가 대학에서 만난 1998년의 세상을. 이런 걸 잊을 수 있으면 얼마나 좋아. 공장들이 문을 닫고 일자리를 잃어선 안 되는 사람들이 거리로 쏟아져 나왔는데, 어디를 가도 그런 행렬을 만날 수 있었다는 사실. 그리고 죽음도.

of comfort, though, and from his aloof expression, I read that he was used to such wretchedness and tired of having to hear about it. Although I was flustered, I kept playing. Come to think of it, however, I had never helped him either when he was unhappy.

The time I spent with him in that café was not all that meaningless though. After all, I wrote this story. To teach me chess, he even made picture cards with the chess pieces on them and explained each one to me. When I got tired of it, as I often do of anything, and said, "Shall we have some fun today, instead of playing chess?" he opened his laptop and said, "Do you want to play a game of chess with a computer then?" Considering this friend, who tried to teach me chess so diligently, I should not say this, but, in fact, I was not paying attention to chess at the time. I was absorbed in something else, especially because the café was located in front of the university from which we had both graduated.

I remembered the same friend talking about poetry when we had been young students at the university. He had shoulder-length hair then and, for some reason, insisted on wearing a long khaki trench coat that came down to his ankles. I also remembered a vivid image of Che Guevara's face

많은 사람들이 그런 방법으로 여기를 빠져 나갔고 우리는 스무 살을 통과해 그때 그들의 나이였을지 모를 나이가 되었는데, 우리는 왜 체스에 대해서는 이야기하지만 마음을 누르는 어떤 불행에 대해서는 솔직히 이야기하고 위안 받지 못할까. 지금도 생각을 한다. 그런 건 왜 그렇게 어려워. 지난 일이니까 지난 일은 지난 일대로 보내야 하는 것일까. 하지만 우리가 어떻게 그럴 수 있을까.

나는 일상을 가만히 살다가도 다른 세계로 가고 싶다는 마음이 들고 그럴 때 대개 글을 쓰는데 그러다 보면 정말 그런 곳을 통과하고 있다는 기분도 든다. 그런 기분으로 가닿는 곳에는 혼자 있는 것이 아니라 다수가, 아는 얼굴뿐만 아니라 모르는 이들까지 한데 모여 있는, 그렇게 해서 하나의 '덩어리'로 만져지는 사람들의 소음이 있고, 「체스의 모든 것」의 마지막을 쓸 때쯤에는 그런 소음들 사이를 통과하는, 2011년 런던에서 들었던 이런 노래가 들려왔다. 그리니치를 갔다가 런던으로 돌아가는 기차에서 나는 뇌성마비를 앓았는지 몸을 심하게 뒤틀고 침을 끊임없이 흘리던 한 백인소년의 맞은편에 앉았는데 소년은 혼자였고 그의 티셔츠가 침에 심

that he had carved in a piece of wood. The South American revolutionary wore a beard and beret, which we said made him look like Jesus Christ. As a matter of fact, I wrote that episode into the first draft of the story, but took it out later.

I had a hard time writing the first part of the story, erasing one draft after another. I don't remember why. But I clearly remember starting to drink ice coffee, because it was already May and the beginning of summer.

While swallowing the cold drink, I felt like pressing down something that kept surging up in me. How wonderful it would be if I could stop thinking about the world we had faced as university students in 1998.[2] I really do wish I could forget all about it. The factories closed and those who feared losing their jobs spilled into the streets. Wherever I went, I witnessed marching crowds, and death too: many people took their own lives. And we have survived through our twenties and become the age they probably were at the time. Now we can talk about chess all we want. Why then can't we have

2) The financial crisis experienced by Korean people from 1997 to 2001, which was caused by the severe foreign exchange shortage. Korea was bailed out by the IMF Standby Credit Facility and had to go through an extensive economic restructuring. By January 1998, thousands of business enterprises were already bankrupt, skyrocketing the unemployment rate, and countless workers suffered from overdue wages.

하게 젖어 들어갔으므로 일행 중 하나가 휴지를 꺼내 이것을 사용해, 하며 친절히 말을 걸었다. '플리즈'라는 말을 붙여 간곡하게. 손가락으로 휴지를 집은 소년은 얼굴을 좀 닦다가 기차가 런던에 도착한다는 방송이 나오자 노래를 불렀는데 런던 브리지 폴링다운, 폴링다운, 폴링다운, 하는 노래였어. 기차는 런던의 템스강을 건너며 그 거리를, 그 오래고 지지 않는 태양의 거리 속으로 진입하는데 나는 소년의 멜로디에 마음을 빼앗겨 다른 것에 대해서는 생각할 수가 없었어. 왕과 여왕과 기사와 주교의 도시, 그곳에서 태어나고 자란 소년이 뒤틀리는 몸으로 마치 축복하듯 혹은 무언가를 강렬히 암시하듯 부르던 노래를.

소설을 쓰면서 이 소설이 독해되지 못할까봐 걱정했다. 소설 안에 어떤 공동(空同)을 만들어놓고 쓰는 것과 같았어. 그것을 절실히 느끼지만 그것에 대해서는 말할 수가 없고, 말을 하려고 할 때마다 소리가 새어나가버려서 도저히 그럴 수는 없고 그것 외의 것들을 말함으로써 그것의 위치를 지정하는 방식. 하지만 생각해보면 그런 공동 덕분에 무언가가 흐르지 않는가 하는 생각이 든다. 공기가 여기서 저기로 그러면 당연히 바람이 불

an honest talk about the wretchedness that is pressing down on our hearts so that we can get some relief? I still think: "Why is it so difficult to talk about things like that? Yes, they are the things of the past. But, is it really okay to simply let them fade away? How could we ever live with that?"

Normally, I go through my everyday routines, uneventfully; but at times, I am attacked by the impulse to travel into another world. In such instances, I usually sit down to write, and, while composing, I sometimes feel like I am actually passing into an unfamiliar world. The feeling conjures up a place where I am not alone, where a large number of people, some of whom I recognize, have congregated. There are also noises produced by this cluster of people, giving a tactile sensation of some kind of a large lump. When I was writing the ending of "Everything About Chess," I also heard a song weaving through these noises; it was a song I had heard in London in 2011. On a train bound from Greenwich to London, I saw a Caucasian boy who was drooling and twisting his body ceaselessly, perhaps because of cerebral palsy. He was sitting opposite me and unaccompanied. His T-shirt was soaking wet with saliva, so a member of our group took out some tissue paper and spoke to him in a cordial tone: "Use this, please, if you want

지, 바람이 불면 소리가 나고 소리라는 것은 음계인데 그러면 그것은 노래로도 읽힐 수 있으니까 우리는 가만히 듣는 것만으로도 많은 것을 말할 수 있다. 어떻게 그러냐고, 글쎄, 하지만 정말 그래, 그 공동에 대해 우리가 아는 것만으로도 충분히 그래. 어떻게 안 그래.

to." The boy received the tissue paper with his fingers and began wiping his face. Then it was announced that the train would soon arrive in London. Upon hearing the announcement, the boy began to sing a song: "London Bridge is falling down, falling down, falling down..." The train crossed the River Thames and entered London, where the sun, the ancient sun of a past empire, was said to never set. Nevertheless, fascinated by the melody of the boy's song, I could not think of anything else. London, the city of kings, queens, knights, and bishops. The boy who was born and grew up in that city was singing the song, his body still twisting, as if blessing or intensely alluding to something.

Writing this story, I was worried that it might not be understood by the reader. It felt like I was creating some sort of a hollowness inside the story. I was sometimes acutely aware of a thought in my mind, but I was unable to write it down. Whenever I attempted to write it, the sound of the thought would slip away from me, forcing me to give up. So, I decided to give the thought its own place, though unspoken, in the story by narrating all the other things. Come to think of it, thanks to that hollow, the unspoken seems to flow through the story. When air flows from here to there, the wind blows, naturally. And the wind makes sounds and the sounds are musical. If so, then the wind or the hollow can be read as a song. That means we can say a lot just by listening. How is it possible? Well, we really can. With only what we already know about the hollow, we most certainly can. How can we not?

해설
Commentary

룰의 세계를 내파하는 사랑의 룰

이선우 (문학평론가)

이미지의 반역, 반역의 이미지

낯익은 파이프 그림, 그 아래 적힌 '이것은 파이프가 아니다'라는 난감한 문구. 널리 알려진 마그리트의 〈이미지의 반역〉이다. 이 작품이 미술사에 뚜렷한 족적을 남길 수 있었던 것은 그림과 모순된 텍스트가 함께 배치되었기 때문이다. 텍스트 자체에 이미 언어와 대상 사이의 필연성을 의심하고 사고의 자동성을 정지시키고자 하는 노림수가 담겨 있지만 이 둘의 결합 덕분에 이미지와 대상, 가상과 실재를 혼동하는 우리의 관습적 사고는 더욱 효과적으로 의심, 전복된다. 그러나 「체스의 모든 것」에서 노아는, 이제 하나의 정전이 되어버린 마그리트

The Rule of Love That Implodes the World of Rules

Lee Sun-woo (literary critic)

Rebellion of the Image, the Image of Rebellion

A familiar painting of a pipe. The enigmatic text under it: "This is not a pipe." It is of course René Magritte's famous work, titled "Rebellion of the Image." The effect of the juxtaposition of the painting and text that contradicts it helped this painting occupy a distinct place in the history of art. In the text itself, one can detect the painter's suspicion about the inevitability of the link between language and object, his effort to put an end to cognitive automatism. Thanks to the juxtaposition of the two, our conventional thought processes, in which we confuse an image with an object, and imagination with reality, becomes suspect and gets subverted. However,

의 〈이미지의 반역〉을 "미술관의 금테가 넝쿨처럼 장식하는 호화로움의 스퀘어 속에" 갇힌 "반역의 이미지", "이해불가능의 자기기만"이라고 몰아세운다.

마그리트는 과연 "가상의 파괴"를 시도한 것일까, 그저 "반역의 이미지화"에 성공한 것일 뿐일까. 아니, 이 둘은 서로 꼬리를 무는 관계다. 가상의 파괴에 성공해야만 반역의 이미지가 될 수 있기 때문이다. 그러나 반역의 이미지가 되는 순간, 그것은 다시 하나의 이미지, 가상이 될 수밖에 없으니 가상의 파괴는 영원히 달성될 수 없는 과제가 된다.

「체스의 모든 것」역시 실패의 기록이다. 그러나 이 작품이 집중하고 있는 것은 가상을 파괴하고자 하는 의지로 충만한 반역자들이 아니라, 어쩔 수 없이 파괴되어가는 가상들의 맨얼굴이다. 반역에도 실패하고, 반역의 이미지에서도 이제 내려와야만 하는 패배자들의 이야기, 하여 군림을 위한 승리가 아니라 스스로에 대한 부끄러움을 '이기는 것에 대한 간절함', 모욕당한 자들의 이 공통감각에 대한 이야기가 소설의 한 축을 형성한다.

in "Everything About Chess," the protagonist Noah berates Magritte's famous painting for being just an "image of rebellion" and the "self-deception of the incomprehensible," confined in its "square of luxury" and nestled in the museum's "gold rim."

Staying with this character's essay discussed within the story, did Magritte indeed attempt the "destruction of the imaginary"? Or did he merely succeed in creating an "image of rebellion"? I believe the two are connected with each other, as in the Möbius strip. Only when the destruction of the imaginary has been successful can an image of rebellion be born. And yet the moment an image of rebellion is born, it is destined to become another image, that is, to become part of the imaginary again. Hence, the destruction of the imaginary becomes a task that can never be accomplished.

"Everything About Chess" is also a record of failure. What this work focuses on, however, is not rebels who are determined to destroy the imaginary, but the bare, mask-less faces of the imaginary in the process of their own inevitable destruction. It is the story of the defeated, those who have failed in their attempts at rebellion and now have no choice but to step down from their throne in the image of rebellion. Therefore, one structural axis of this work is formed by the feelings shared

개개의 진실, 실존을 위한 사투

마그리트의 〈이미지의 반역〉에 대한 싱반된 평가처럼 이 소설의 인물들이 서로를 바라보는 시선에도 다양한 온도차가 존재한다. 일테면 노아에 대한 '나'와 국화의 상이한 관점, 국화에 대한 '나'와 노아의 다른 감각. 동일한 인물과 사건에 대한 다층적 시선, 해석의 충돌은 이 소설을 구성하는 핵심원리다. 보는 사람에 의해서만 해석이 달라지는 것이 아니다. 시간도 생각의 변화를 낳는다. 관점을 바꿀만한 새로운 사실이 드러나기도 하고, 세월에 따라 인물 자체의 변화가 수반되기도 한다. 그렇게 이 소설은 하나의 진실을 향해서가 아니라 각자의 진실, 진실의 모든 것을 향한다.

노아 선배를 중심으로 '나'와 국화가 이루는 삼각구도를 보자. '나'에게 노아 선배는, 일상적인 일들에 서투르지만 서툴러서 못한다기보다는 '다르게 하는' 인물이다. 그 '다름'이 나를 매료시킨다. 어쩌면 우울증과 정동 장애를 앓고 있는 것까지, '내'가 노아에게서 발견한 '다름'의 목록들은 모두 그를 "힙하고 쿨한 우울한 청춘"의 표상으로 만들기에 부족함이 없었을 것이다. 하여 '나'는 "어딘가 다른 중력에서 사는 듯한" 그를 "그냥 '그렇다'고 있

by the insulted—as opposed to domineering vic-
tors—and their dire need to "conquer their own
sense of humiliation."

Individual Truth, Desperate Struggle for Existence

Like the contradicting appreciations of Magritte's
"Rebellion of the Image," the characters in this story
see one another from different points of view. For
example, the narrator and Kuk-hwa observe Noah
from their own perspectives. Likewise, the feelings
of the narrator and Noah towards Kuk-hwa con-
tradict each other. The essential principle at work
throughout the story is multiple viewpoints of the
same character and events or the conflicting interpretations of them. The different interpretations
stem not only from different characters but also
from the passage of time. A new fact is revealed to
change the point of view, and as time passes,
characters themselves change. Thus, the story
moves not towards one ultimate truth, but towards
individual truths or all truths.

Let us take a look at the triangular relationship of
Noah, the narrator, and Kuk-hwa, with Noah at the
center of this triangulation. According to the narrator, Noah is clumsy in his everyday life, not because he doesn't know how to deal with it, but be-

는 그대로" 받아들이게 되고, 이 "새로운 감각" 속에서 그의 곁을 맴돈다. 그러나 노아가 집착하는 것은, 그를 배려하고 이해하고 걱정하는 '나'가 아니라 막무가내로 억지를 부려 그를 항상 실패로 몰아넣는 국화다.

선배에 대한 최소한의 예의는커녕 때로는 공격적일 정도의 무심함까지 발산하는 국화에게 노아는 왜 모든 것을 참아내며 다가가려 하는 것일까. 노아에게는 국화가 바로 '반역의 이미지'이기 때문이다. '내'가 노아의 '다름'에서 청춘의 새로운 감각을 맛보았던 것처럼, 노아는 자신과 달리 타인에게 무심하고 세상의 룰에 전혀 굴하지 않는 국화야말로 이 세계의 승자로 자리매김할 수 있는 반역의 아이콘이라 여겼을 법하다. 서로 다른 방향을 바라보고 있지만, 그러므로 이들이 욕망하는 것은 결국 같은 이미지이다.

그러나 국화의 단순한 동선이 드러내는 것은, 그녀가 단지 '자유분방하고 쿨한 20대'가 아니라 산다는 것의 비참을 억척스럽게 감내하고 있는 고학생이라는 사실이다. 점심은 언제나 학생식당에서만 먹으면서도 하루도 빠짐없이 각종 아르바이트를 하고 틈틈이 학업에도 매진해야 하는 국화로서는 반역의 '이미지' 따위나 연출하

cause he deals with it "in unfamiliar ways." The narrator is attracted to his unfamiliarity—and even his melancholia and manic-depressive psychosis. The long list of Noah's idiosyncrasies is more than enough for the narrator to worship him as an emblem of "melancholy youth who are hip and cool." The narrator decides to accept Noah, who seems to live "in another gravity zone," just the way he is. The new feelings she experiences around him pull her towards him like a magnet. Unfortunately for her, though, the person Noah is infatuated with is not the narrator who understands and worries about him, but their mutual friend Kuk-hwa whose obstinacy makes him feel defeated.

Why is Noah attracted to Kuk-hwa, who is so ill-mannered towards him and who feels no qualms about being aggressively callous towards him? What compels him to be patient with her and to wish to stay close to her? Is it because in Noah's eyes, Kuk-hwa is the "image of rebellion"? As Noah's idiosyncrasies give new and youthful feelings to the narrator, Kuk-hwa's heedlessness to others, unfamiliar as it may be to him, and her refusal to succumb to the rules of the world make Noah see her as an icon of rebellion that deserves the status of an ultimate winner in the world. All three characters' attraction may be for different

고 있는 노아가 "유아적"으로 보일 수밖에 없다. 그는 15세기에 만들어진 체스의 신사적인 룰이나 네 것 내 것 구분 없이 쌓아놓고 혼자 먹어버리는 감자튀김, 잔돈 몇 푼 따위는 돌려주지 않아도 그만이라고 생각하는 노아의 무신경한 태도에서조차 민감하게 "언페어"를 감지하는 인물인 것이다. 문맹의 부모를 둔 국화에게 세상은 처음부터 공정한 게임이 아니었을 것이다. '나'는 국화를 '부주의하게' '천연덕스럽게' '무심한' '공격적인' 등의 부정적 어휘로 수식하지만, 국화의 이런 태도는 타고난 품성이 아니라 이 불공정한 게임에서 살아남기 위한 일종의 전략이 아니었을까.

'이기는 사람이 되겠다'는 국화의 다짐이 단순히 세속적 성공이나 출세를 의미하는 것이 아니라 부끄러움을 이기는 사람, "부끄러우면 부끄러운 상태로 그걸 넘어서는 사람"이라는 점은 그래서 더욱 많은 생각을 하게 만든다. 70년대에 박완서는 '부끄러움을 가르칩니다'라는 제목의 소설로 중산층의 속물성을 날카롭게 파헤쳤다. 40년이 지났다. 많은 기성세대들이 여전히 부끄러움을 모른 채 살아가고 있지만, 구조적으로 경제적 자립과 사회 진출이 가로막힌 상당수의 청년세대는 모멸감에 허

people, but in the end, they desire the same thing.

However, Kuk-hwa's weekly routine reveals that she is not just an "unrestricted and cool woman in her twenties," but also a self-supporting student who is doggedly enduring a wretchedness in life. She always eats lunch at the student cafeteria, has various part-time jobs every day, and has to catch up with her studies whenever she has time. So, in Kuk-hwa's eyes, Noah, who is bent on producing a mere "image" of rebellion is "childish." Kuk-hwa sensitively perceives the "unfairness" in the gentlemanly rules of chess, established back in the 15th century, that Noah follows, and in his callousness, for example, when he eats up a pile of French fries meant for all three of them, or when he doesn't share small change. The world is not a fair place from the beginning for Kuk-hwa, who has illiterate parents. The narrator describes Kuk-hwa in negative words such as "carelessly," "nonchalantly," "heedless," and "aggressive." But Kuk-hwa's behavior may not reflect her innate personality, but instead be a kind of strategy for surviving the unfair games of the world.

By her stated resolve "to be a conqueror," Kuk-hwa explains that she does not mean mundane success or climbing up the social hierarchy. Rather, she means "a person who can overcome shame

덕인다. 실질적 대책도 시급하지만, 이제 부끄러움이 아니라 부끄러움을 이기는 것에 대해서도 함께 고민해야 하는 시대가 온 것이다. 외적인 조건들이 무참히 짓밟아버린 인간의 존엄성, 그것을 다시 회복시키지 않는 한 우리가 다음 세대에 기대할 수 있는 것은 많지 않다.

"국화는 냉정하고 무심하니까 얼마든지 그럴 수 있으리라 생각"한 '나'와 달리 노아가 국화의 저 말에 유난히 감동해 오랫동안 응원한 것은, "이기는 사람"에 대한 간절함과 실감이 '나'와는 달랐기 때문이다. '나'는 한참 뒤에야 알게 된 노아의 모멸감. 벗어나고 싶을수록 오히려 자기를 학대하고 말았던 그 자멸의 시간 동안 노아는 대신 이겨줄 누군가라도 간절히 소망했을 것이다. 누군가의 승리가 곧 나의 승리는 아닐지라도 적어도 하나의 가능성은 될 수 있으니까. 이렇게 사람들은 우상을 만들고 가상의 이미지에 빠져든다. 쉽게 비판할 수 있다. 그러나 실재를 보지 못하는 자들의 나약함에 대해 비판할 때 우리는 그 고통의 크기와 절박함에 대해서는 곧잘 침묵한다.

"나는 걔가 이기는 사람이 되라고 응원해, 정말 확실히 그렇게 될 수 있을 거라고 생각해, 거기에는 아무런 의

while accepting shame as part of herself." It is quite a thought-provoking sentence. In the 1970s, Park Wan-sŏ wrote a short story entitled, "To Teach Shame," which scrutinizes the snobbism of the middle class. Forty years have passed since then. Many people of the older generation still live without even thinking about shame. However, a large number of people of the younger generation—who have been denied economic independence and social advancement due to structural problems of society—suffer from a sense of humiliation. Of course, some practical measures are urgently needed. Nevertheless, it is also time to think deeply about not only shame but also how to overcome it. Unless we restore the dignity of humanity, which has been trampled by external conditions, there is not much we can expect of the coming generations.

"[A]ware of her cool-headedness and heedlessness, [the narrator] believed [Kuk-hwa] could easily make herself a conqueror of any kind." Noah is more profoundly touched by Kuk-hwa's wish and roots for her for a long time. The reason for this difference between the narrator and Noah is clear: Unlike the narrator, Noah identifies himself with Kuk-hwa and desperately wants to be a "conqueror of shame" himself. The narrator learns of the

심이 없다고 생각해. 하지만 나는 앞으로 걔를 볼 수 없을 거라고 예상해, 그것은 어떤 오류의 가능성 없이 확실해." 영어문장을 그대로 번역한 저 어색한 문투와 거기서 생겨난 야릇한 운율, '생각하다' '예상하다' '확실하다'처럼 감정과는 무관한 건조한 술어가 에워싸고 있는 절절한 문장들. 형식과 내용의 낙차가 묘한 울림을 주는 저 복문들처럼, 국화와 노아는 겉으로 드러난 이미지와는 달리 거창하게 이 세계에 반역을 꾀한 것이 아니라 매순간 자기 자신의 실존과 사투를 벌이고 있었던 것은 아닐까. 이 비정한 세계에서 얼마나 더 수치스럽게 삶을 이어가야 할 것인가, 하고. 그러나 부끄러움을 이기는 일은, 아이러니하지만 바로 이런 질문으로부터 시작하는 것이다. 이들을 아직 패배자라 부를 수 없는 이유다.

룰의 세계를 내파하는 사랑의 룰

「체스의 모든 것」은 이 모든 것을 치밀하게 구조화하면서도 그 뼈대를 쉽게 노출시키지 않는 의뭉함으로도 탁월하지만, 소설의 주제가 하나로 일목요연하게 꿰어지지 않는다는 점에서 더욱 매력적인 작품이다. 각자가 바라본 상대의 일면이 그 인물의 모든 것이 아니었던 것

humiliation Noah has suffered. The more desperate Noah wants to emerge from the sense of humiliation, the more cruel he becomes to himself. At the time of self-destruction, Noah perhaps wishes in earnest for someone else to conquer shame on behalf of him. Someone else's triumph may not be his to enjoy, yet it can at least show him the possibility. Thus people create an idol and fall for the false image, the imaginary. It is easy to criticize these people. However, when we criticize the weakness of those who cannot see reality, we tend to keep silent about the severity and urgency of their pain.

"I think she will be that kind of conqueror. And I'm rooting for her to be one," Noah asserts. "I truly believe she can be such a person. I have no doubts about it. But I also believe I won't be able to see her ever again. It's a fact, with no room for errors." The translation of Noah's article from English into Korean causes the awkward tone in these sentences. And yet there is some subtle meter and a sense of appropriateness to them, dotted with dry-sounding, free-of-emotion expressions like "think," "no doubts," and "no room for errors." Like these complex sentences with their odd resonances, stemming from the discrepancy between the form and the content, Kuk-hwa and Noah, unlike their

처럼, 이 소설이 품고 있는 일견 모순적인 이야기들은 오히려 소설의 결을 풍성하게 만들며 여러 가지 질문들을 제출한다.

일테면, '나'가 노아에게, 노아가 국화에게 끌리게 된 것이 반역의 이미지, 곧 상대의 실재가 아니라 가상이었을 뿐이라고 해서 이들의 사랑을 사랑이 아니었다고 잘라 말할 수 있을 것인가. 이제 '반역의 이미지'가 어떻게 "기대를 배반한 반역"에 머물고 말았는지를, 반역 따위는 언감생심, 실은 그 모든 것이 살아남기 위한 안간힘, "이기는 것에 대한 간절함"이 만든 포즈에 불과했다는 것을 알게 된 삼십 대가 되었다. 뿐인가, 그들 앞에 놓인 현실은 점점 더 나빠지는 것만 같다. 누군가는 사랑을 잃었고 누군가는 이혼했다. 우울증이 심해졌고, 회사를 그만뒀고, 사업이 망해 죽고 싶을 정도로 지긋지긋하게 빚에 시달리기도 했다. 문자 삐삐 따위와는 비교할 수 없을 정도로 뛰어난 기능의 스마트폰을 너나없이 들고 다니게 되었지만 기술의 진보가 모든 사람들에게 진보였던 것은 아니다. 아픈 사람은 더 아프고 소외되는 사람들은 여전히 소외된다. 자살방지를 위한 핫라인에서조차 매뉴얼대로 주민등록번호를 묻는 이 '룰의 세계'는

external images as larger-than-life heroes conspiring in a rebellion against the whole world, may have been struggling to survive every minute, asking themselves, "How much longer do I have to suffer a life of humiliation in this heartless world?" Nevertheless, the process of conquering shame, ironically, begins with a question like this. That is why they should not to be seen as losers yet.

The Rule of Love That Implodes the World of Rules

"Everything About Chess" has all of the discussion above meticulously woven into its narrative structure, and yet cleverly keeps the structural framework hidden. Perhaps, the fact that the theme of the story is not evident is what gives the work its appeal. As each character's limited understanding of the other two piques our curiosity, the seemingly self-contradicting narrative enriches the story all the more and stimulates a variety of questions for us readers.

For example, can we rule that the narrator's love for Noah and Noah's love for Kuk-hwa are not real love because they are attracted to the mere image of rebellion, not to the reality of their lovers? And now that they are in their thirties and realize that the "image of rebellion" has settled into a "rebellion that be-

가히 공포스러울 정도다.

누아는 어렵사리 다시 국회를 만나 체스를 두지만 새 회를 오래 이어가지 못한다. 중개자였던 '나' 역시 이제 노아로부터 멀어지려고 하고 있다. 이것이 "가상의 파괴"가 가져온 쓸쓸한 결말인 것일까? 르네 지라르는 욕망의 삼각형에서 비롯한 낭만적 거짓을 폭로하고 소설적 진실을 드러내는 것이 위대한 소설의 결말이라고 했다. 단편이지만,「체스의 모든 것」은 소설의 제요소를 동원해 한때 우리를 사로잡았던 가상의 파괴로 치밀하게 나아간다. 그러나 종교적 초월이나 허무로 치닫지도, 가상이 파괴되는 그 순간에 소설을 충격적으로 끝맺지도 않는다. 시간이 흐른 뒤 다시 만난 노아 선배는 "확실히 전보다 더 심각한 상황"에 놓여 있었고, 그와 헤어진 뒤 '나'는 "선배를 보면서 느꼈던 새로운 감각 같은 건 다 어디로 간 것일까?" 슬퍼하지만 "그 뒤로 선배를 자주" 만난다. 말하자면 이 소설은, 가상의 파괴까지가 아니라 그 이후에 대해 생각하는 소설이다. 가상의 이미지에서 시작했다면 가상이 파괴된 순간, 그 관계는 파국을 맞아야 마땅하다. 물론 이들은 서로에게서 "점점 멀어지는 거리를 열심히 계산하면서" 달린다, 도망친다. 선배가 국

trays expectations," and see that they in fact would not dare dream of a rebellion, and that their tough appearance is nothing but a pose born of their struggle to survive, their reality becomes a "desperate wish to conquer shame." Moreover, the reality unfolding before their eyes seems to get worse. One has lost her lover; another has gotten divorced, suffered a worsening case of depression, and quit his job; and yet another has failed in business, gotten harassed with debts, and entertained suicidal thoughts. Everyone can afford a smart phone, whose functions are incomparably better than the text beepers of the past. Yet this technological advance has not led to a better life for society as a whole. Sick people suffer more and alienated people remain alienated. Even a suicide prevention hot line follows the manual blindly and asks first for the caller's resident registration number. And this world of blind rules is indeed appalling.

Noah finally reunites with Kuk-hwa, with difficulty, but their renewed relationship does not last long. The narrator, who plays a crucial role in their reuniting, also feels like distancing herself from Noah. Is this the tragic denouement brought about by the "destruction of the imaginary"? René Girard, in his *Triangle of the Desire*, says that the denouement of great novels is to reveal the novelistic truth

화와의 "재회를 계속 이어가지 못했을 때 우리의 관계도 완전히 끝이 났다고 생각했다."던 브리지 폴링다운, 폴링다운……, 부랑자의 노랫소리가 음울하게 환기시키고 있는 것처럼 이들은 모두 무너지고 있는 세계 속에서 여전히 패배하며 서로에게 불안을 전염시킬 뿐일 테니까.

그러나 '나'에게는 선배가 불러일으켰던 '새로운 감각'에 대한 경도만이 아니라 또다른 감각적 본능이 있다. 타인의 불안에 전염되고 싶지 않다는 이기적인 생각을 실천하는 와중에도 "끊임없이 나를 일깨우며 선배에게 무슨 말을, 아무 말이라도 해야 한다고 충동질"하는 저 '윤리적 감각', 하여 '나'는 "아무리 체스에 대해 말한다 해도 결국 아무것도 달라지지는 않으리라 독하게 생각하면서도" 혹한의 밤에 홀로 걷고 있는 노아에게 위로의 말을, 실패는 아니었다는 말을 멈추지 않는다. "아니 그렇지는 않았어." "아니야, 한심했어." "아니 그렇지는 않았어. 그 정도는 아니었어."

실패를 선언하는 노아와 그것을 부정하는 '나'. 그러나 노아와 국화의 체스가 사랑의 알레고리란 점에서 '나'의 말은 단순한 위로만이 아니다. 체스의 룰에 대한 논쟁

by exposing the romantic lies that stem from the triangle of desire. Although it is a short story, "Everything About Chess" mobilizes all these elements of fiction to meticulously guide the narrative towards the destruction of the false image that has once occupied our minds. Nonetheless, the final destination is not religious transcendence nor nihilism, nor the shock effect at the moment of the destruction of the imaginary. When the narrator finally meets Noah again, after a long period of lost contact, she notices that he is "definitely in a much more serious situation than before." After their meeting, she wonders, "Where have all the fresh sensations gone? Those Noah helped me experience years ago?" And after that, she meets Noah "quite often." In a nutshell, this story aims to show not the destruction of the false image per se, but what is beyond the moment of such a destruction. If the story began only with the motif of the false image, the characters' relationships would naturally come to an end at the moment the false image gets destroyed. Of course, the characters are running, escaping from one another, "calculating the growing distance away from" one another. "I thought my relationship with [Noah] ended for good... when he failed to keep his renewed relationship with her." "London Bridge is falling down, falling down...," as

에서조차 국화의 억지가 노아의 논리를 일방적으로 이겼던 것처럼 다시 만난 뒤에도 노아의 "이상한 패배"는 계속되었을 것이다. "열띠면서도 무시무시하게 공허한" 대화, 대화의 내용보다는 대화에 대한 의지, 대화를 한다는 사실 자체가 대화의 목적인 대화란 바로 사랑의 대화일 텐데, 사랑이라는 게임에서는 더 많이 사랑하는 사람이 질 수밖에 없기 때문이다. 그것이 세상의 룰과는 다른 사랑의 룰이다. 그렇다면, 더 많이 사랑한 것을 과연 실패라고 할 수 있을까. 사랑의 목적이 상대를 소유하거나 사랑을 돌려받는 데 있는 것이 아니라 사랑함 그 자체에 있다면, 사랑에 성공한 것은 더 많이 사랑한 사람이다. '지는 것이 이기는 것'이라는 모순된 명제가 여기서 성립한다. 그러므로 "아니 그렇지는 않았어."라는 '나'의 반복된 부정은, 상대를 위로하기 위한 빈말이 아니라 오히려 진실에 다가서는 말이다. 노아에게만이 아니다. 그것은 노아를 좋아했지만 애초에 그의 상대가 되지 못했고, 하여 항상 비켜서서 관찰하거나 중개하는 역할만 해야 했던 '나' 스스로까지도 긍정하게 만드는 부정. 실패를 거듭하며 체스 두는 방법을 다 배운 뒤에도 국화의 연락처를 수소문해 노아에게 가르쳐주고, 기

the bum's gloomy crooning suggests, and so they would end up only being constantly defeated and spreading anxiety to one another in the midst of a collapsing world.

Fortunately, though, the narrator is given a sensory instinct, in addition to an inclination for the "new feelings" that she feels around Noah. While selfishly refusing to be contaminated by the others' anxiety, her ethical sensitiveness ceaselessly urges her "to talk to Noah, about something, anything." In the end, "although I was unflinchingly convinced that no matter how much we talked about chess, nothing would ever change," she lends Noah, who is walking all alone in the severe cold outside at night, words of comfort, repeatedly telling him that he is not a failure.

"No, you weren't wrong."

"Yes, I was. I was completely hopeless."

"No, you weren't wrong. At least, not to that extent."

Noah declares his own defeat and the narrator denies his declaration. Considering the chess games played by Noah and Kuk-hwa as an allegory of their love for each other, there is more to the narrator's words of comfort than meets the eye. Since Kuk-hwa's stubbornness one-sidedly beats Noah's logic in all of their debates about the chess

껏 매정하게 돌아선 뒤에도 끝내 전화를 걸어 그의 한기(寒氣)에 온기를 더하고야 만 '나'의 바보 같은 사랑 역시 긍정하려는 부정인 것이다.

같은 말을 반복하는 것은 "구제불능의 술꾼"들만이 아니다. 사랑하는 자들도 사랑한다는 말을 끊임없이 반복한다. 가상이 파괴되고 드러난 맨얼굴, 패배한 자들의 한심하고 고통스런 얼굴에서 끝내 고개를 돌리지 않는 자의 서늘한 마음 한편에는 스스로에 대한 연민만이 아니라 그 어떤 논리로도 설명할 수 없는 구제불능의 사랑이 존재한다. 인간의 존엄이 사라진 이 시대에 그것은 인간이 인간에게 보여줄 수 있는 최고의 윤리적 감각일지도 모른다. "주체의 후퇴는 사랑에 본질적이다." 그러나 이러한 "사랑만이 대화적인 것에, 타자에 다가갈 수 있다."[1] 끝없는 패배 속에서도 삶을 지속시키는 힘은, '룰의 세계'에 갇히지 않고 그것을 안으로부터 내파시키는 이 사랑의 룰에서 비롯하는 것이 아닐까.

---

1) 한병철, 『아름다움의 구원』(문학과지성사, 2016)에서 "주체의 후퇴는 정의에 본질적이다." "감정만이 대화적인 것에, 타자에 다가갈 수 있다."라는 문장을 인용해 변용함.

rules, Noah's unreasonable defeat is very likely to continue even after their reunion. Their "at once so heated and terribly empty" dialogs signify their will to dialog rather than the dialog itself; in other words, the fact that they are engaged with each other is the objective of the dialog. If so, there is only one kind of dialog like that: the dialog between lovers. In the dialog of love, the one who loves the other more is bound to lose. That is what makes the rules of love different from those of the world. Can we indeed say "loving the other more" is a failure? If the goal of love is loving in and of itself, rather than owning one's lover or having the same degree of love returned, then the "winner" is the one who loves his/her lover more, hence, an oxymoron: Losing is winning. Therefore, the narrator's repetition of a negation, "No, you weren't wrong," is not just an empty expression to comfort Noah, but a step towards the truth. Her step towards truths does not apply only to her relationship with Noah. She adores Noah, but she also knows that Kuk-hwa is more than a match for her, so she has no choice but to remain an observer or a go-between. Seen in this context, her repetition of the negation is not only to affirm Noah but an affirmation of herself as well. Even after learning the chess rules by losing so many games, she finds out Kuk-hwa's whereabouts and gives Noah her phone number. Even after resolutely turning her back on him, she ends up calling him again to blanket his chill with her warmth. The narrator's seemingly foolish love for Noah is also her way of affirming herself.

Repeating oneself is not only done by "irredeemable drunkards." Lovers also constantly repeat "I love you" to each other. Hidden inside the heart of someone who refuses to turn away from the pathetic, pain-stricken face of the defeated, after the mask of the imaginary is stripped away, is not only compassion for oneself but the "irredeemable" love for others that no logic can explain. It may be the highest level of ethical sensitivity that one human can exercise on another in this day and age, in which the dignity of humanity is fading away. "The retreat of the subject is essential to love." However, this kind of "love alone can approach the dialogical, the Other."[1]The strength that sustains life even in the midst of endless defeat derives from the rule of love that does not imprison itself in a world of rules, but instead destroys that world from within.

1) Pyong-chol Han, *Redeeming Beauty*, Seoul: Moonji Publishing, 2016. The quoted sentence is a transfiguration of two sentences from *Redeeming Beauty*: "The retreat of the subject is essential to justice"; "Emotions alone can approach the dialogical, the Other."

비평의 목소리
Critical Acclaim

우리 시대의 감정생태에 대한 공시적 시각과, 그러한 감정생태를 초래한 한국사회를 조망하는 통시적 시각을 두루 갖춘 김금희의 소설세계가 많은 독자들과 만나기를 바란다.

신샛별, 「우리 시대의 감정생태 보고서」, 《문학동네》, 2016

김금희의 문장들은 촌(村)스럽다. 그것은 세련되지 않고 어리숙하다는 뜻이 아니라, 도시를 경제적, 문화적 기준으로 살아가는 사람들이 이제는 자신의 것이 아니라고 상심하는 감성의 어떤 부분을 자극한다는 점에서 그렇다.

서희원, 「반복과 망각」, 《현대문학》, 2016

The chronotopes of Kim Keum-hee's fiction illuminate at once the contemporary mode of emotional life and the society that has given rise to it. I hope many readers will have a chance to experience Kim Keum-hee's original world of fiction.

Shin Saet-pyol, "Report on the Emotional Ecology of Our Time," *Munhakdongne*, 2016

Kim Keum-hee's sentences are rustic. I do not mean that they are unrefined or naive, but that they stimulate a particular sensitivity that is now considered lost, and that is grieved over by those whose economic and cultural lives are defined by metropolitan standards.

So Hui-won, "Repetition and Oblivion," *Hyundae Munhak*, 2016

K-픽션 016
체스의 모든 것

2016년 11월 11일 초판 1쇄 발행

지은이 김금희 | **옮긴이** 전미세리 | **펴낸이** 김재범
기획위원 전성태, 정은경, 이경재
편집 윤단비, 김형욱 | **관리** 강초민 | **디자인** 나루기획
인쇄·제책 AP프린팅 | **종이** 한솔PNS
펴낸곳 (주)아시아 | **출판등록** 2006년 1월 27일 제406-2006-000004호
주소 경기도 파주시 회동길 445(서울 사무소: 서울특별시 동작구 서달로 161-1 3층)
전화 02.821.5055 | **팩스** 02.821.5057 | **홈페이지** www.bookasia.org
ISBN 979-11-5662-173-7(set) | 979-11-5662-298-7(04810)
값은 뒤표지에 있습니다.

K-Fiction 016
Everything About Chess

Written by Kim Keum-hee I **Translated by** Jeon Miseli
Published by ASIA Publishers I 445, Hoedong-gil, Paju-si, Gyeonggi-do, Korea
(Seoul Office:161-1, Seodal-ro, Dongjak-gu, Seoul, Korea)
Homepage Address www.bookasia.org I **Tel**. (822).821.5055 I **Fax**. (822).821.5057
First published in Korea by ASIA Publishers 2016
ISBN 979-11-5662-173-7(set) | 979-11-5662-298-7(04810)

바이링궐 에디션 한국 대표 소설

한국문학의 가장 중요하고 첨예한 문제의식을 가진 작가들의 대표작을 주제별로 선정!
하버드 한국학 연구원 및 세계 각국의 한국문학 전문 번역진이 참여한 번역 시리즈!
미국 하버드대학교와 컬럼비아대학교 동아시아학과, 캐나다 브리티시컬럼비아대학교 아시아
학과 등 해외 대학에서 교재로 채택!